# Pea, Bee, & Jay
## LIFT OFF

## Brian "Smitty" Smith

HARPER alley

An Imprint of HarperCollinsPublishers

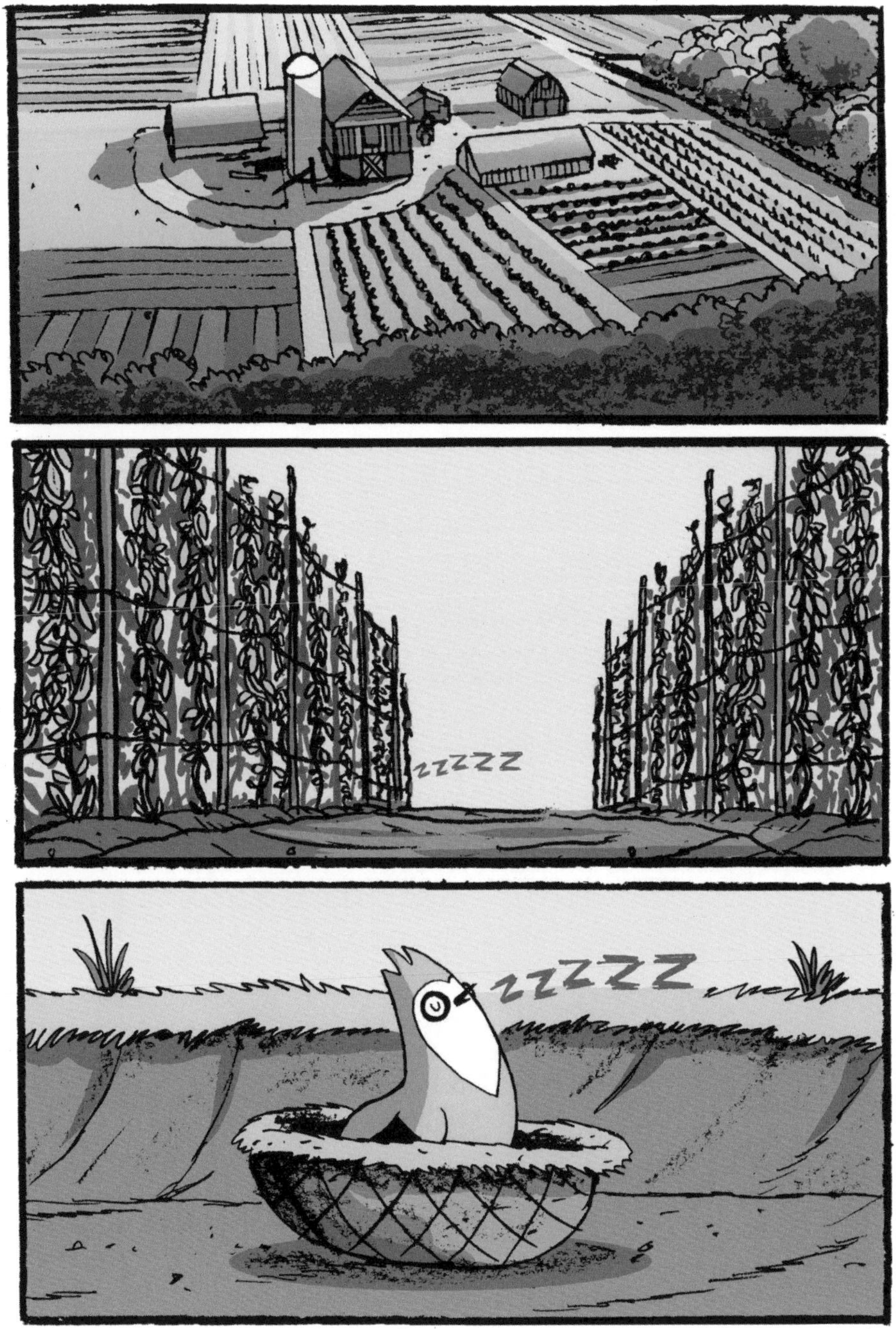
zzzzz
zzzzz

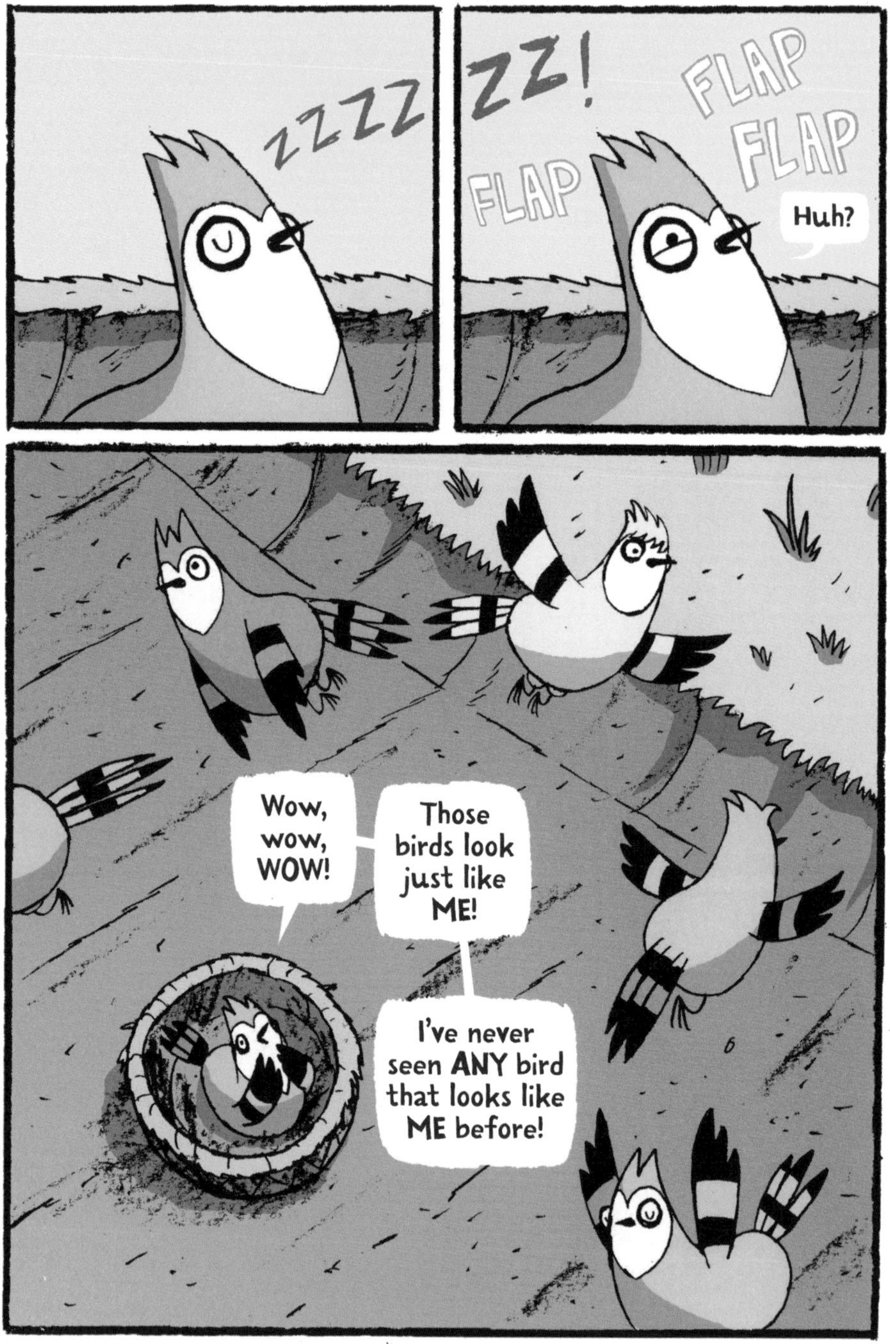
ZZZZZ ZZ!
FLAP
FLAP
FLAP
Huh?
Wow, wow, WOW!
Those birds look just like ME!
I've never seen ANY bird that looks like ME before!

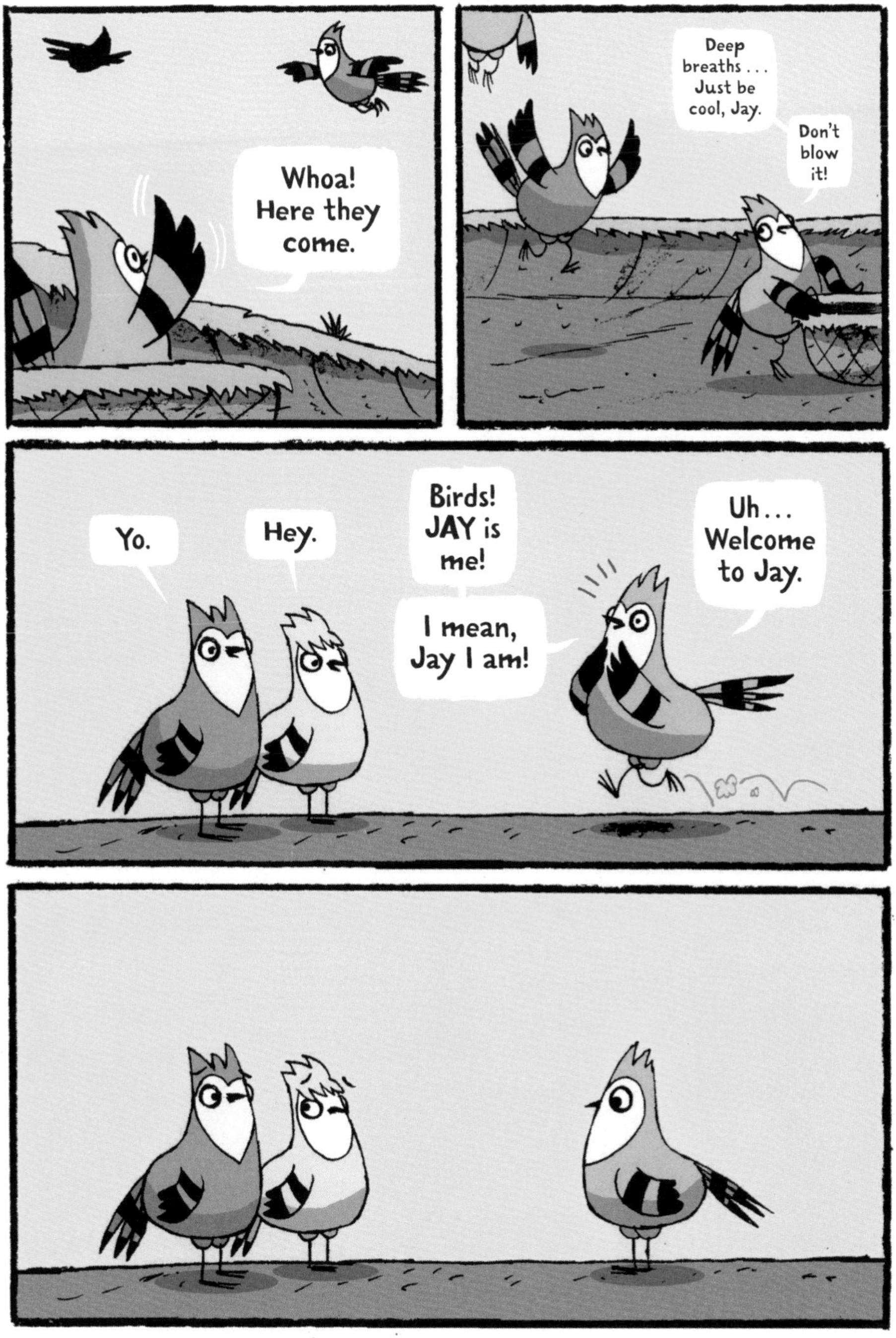
Whoa!
Here they come.
Deep breaths . . . Just be cool, Jay.
Don't blow it!
Yo.
Hey.
Birds! JAY is me!
I mean, Jay I am!
Uh . . . Welcome to Jay.

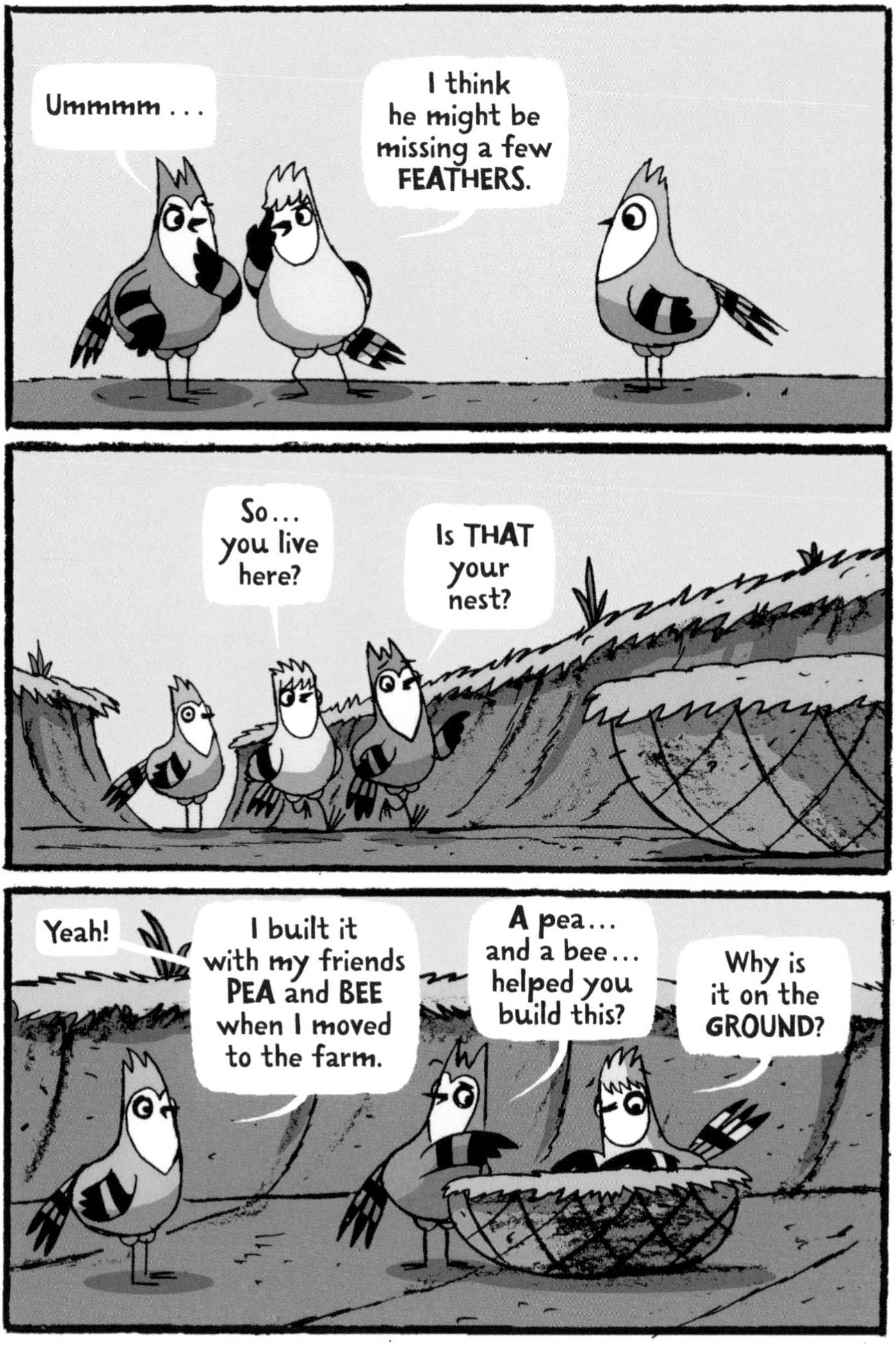
Ummmm . . .
I think he might be missing a few FEATHERS.
So... you live here?
Is THAT your nest?
Yeah!
I built it with my friends PEA and BEE when I moved to the farm.
A pea... and a bee... helped you build this?
Why is it on the GROUND?

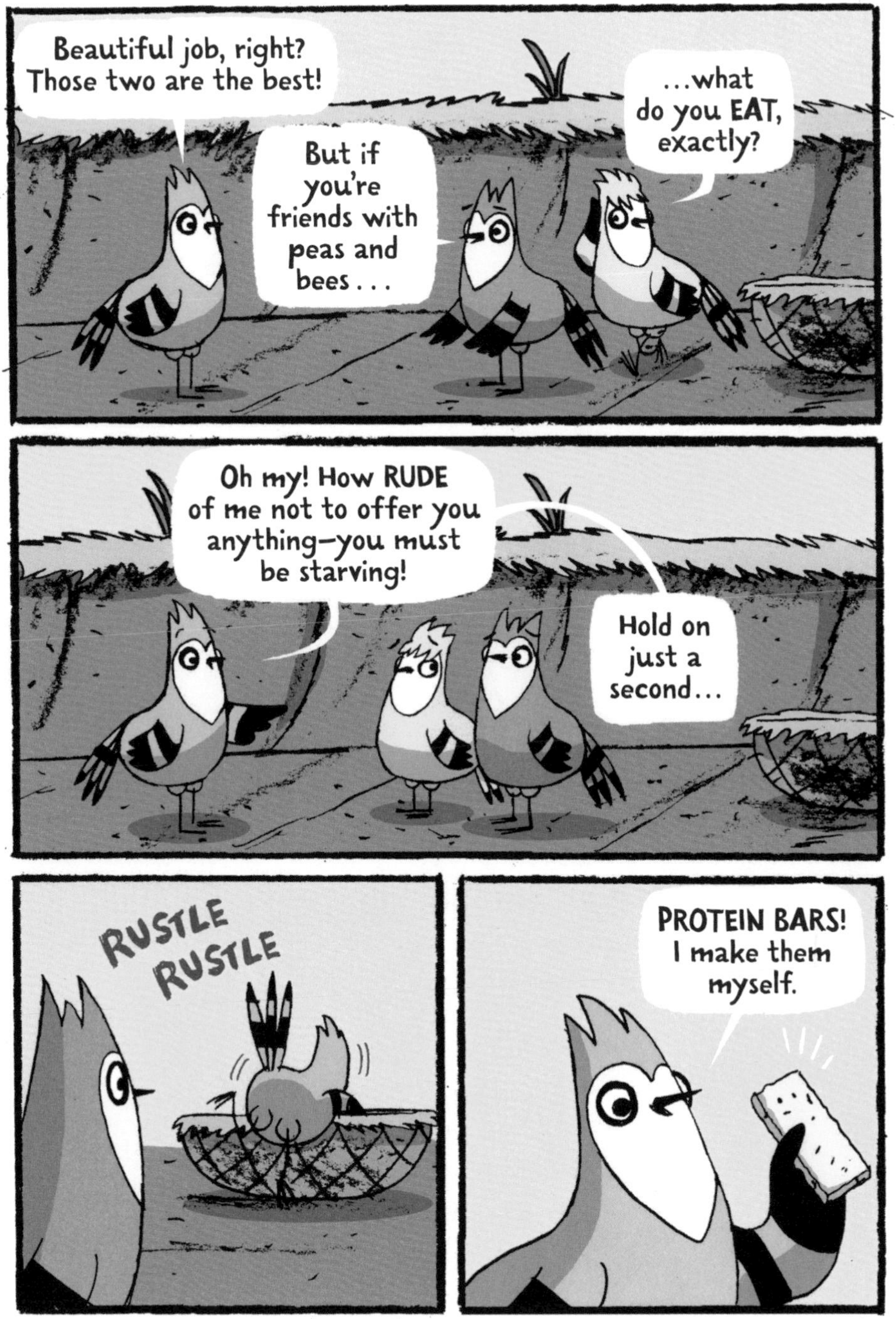
Beautiful job, right? Those two are the best!
But if you're friends with peas and bees . . .
. . . what do you EAT, exactly?
Oh my! How RUDE of me not to offer you anything—you must be starving!
Hold on just a second . . .
RUSTLE RUSTLE
PROTEIN BARS! I make them myself.

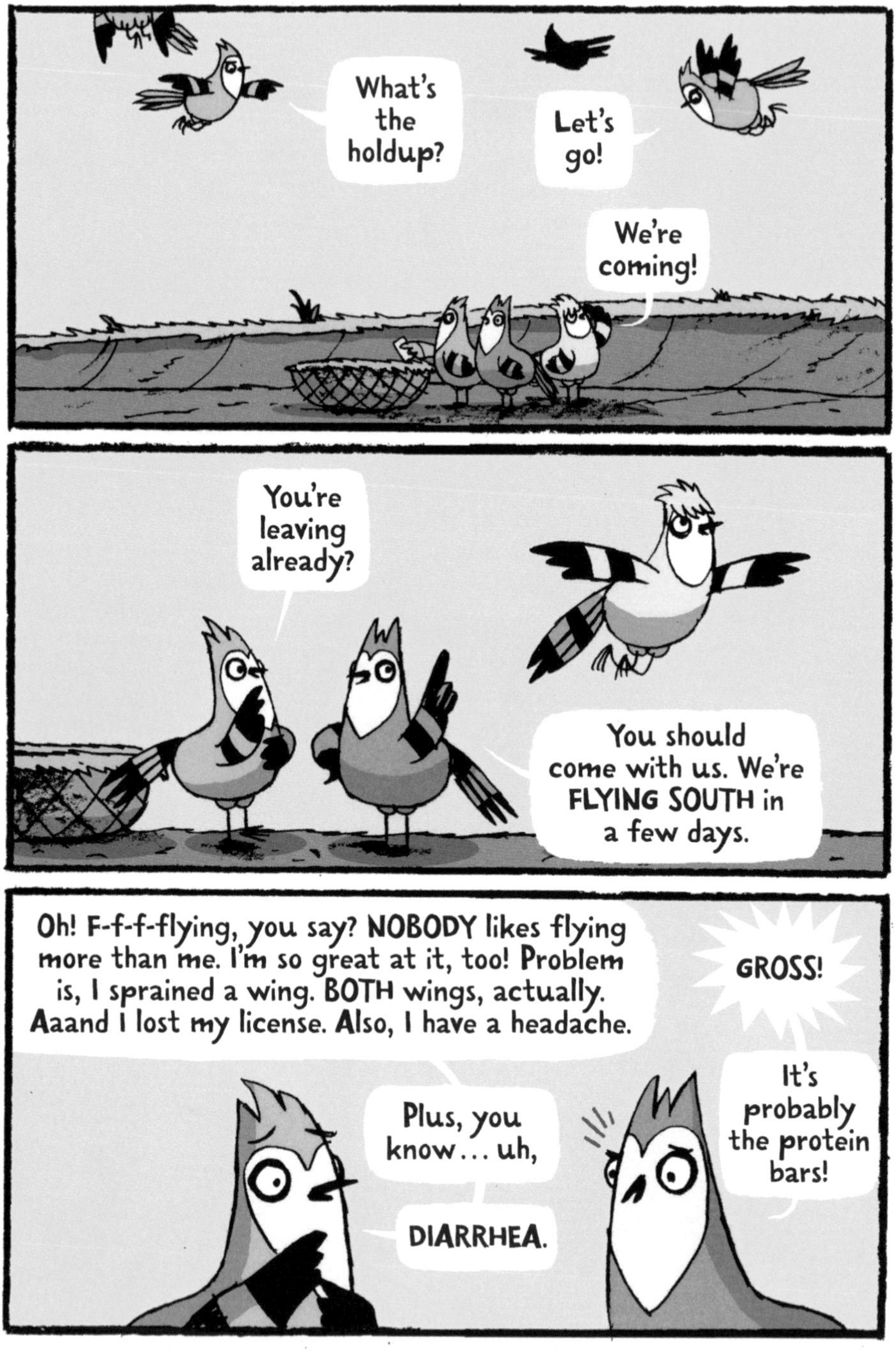
What's the holdup?
Let's go!
We're coming!
You're leaving already?
You should come with us. We're FLYING SOUTH in a few days.
Oh! F-f-f-flying, you say? NOBODY likes flying more than me. I'm so great at it, too! Problem is, I sprained a wing. BOTH wings, actually. Aaand I lost my license. Also, I have a headache.
Plus, you know… uh,
DIARRHEA.
GROSS!
It's probably the protein bars!

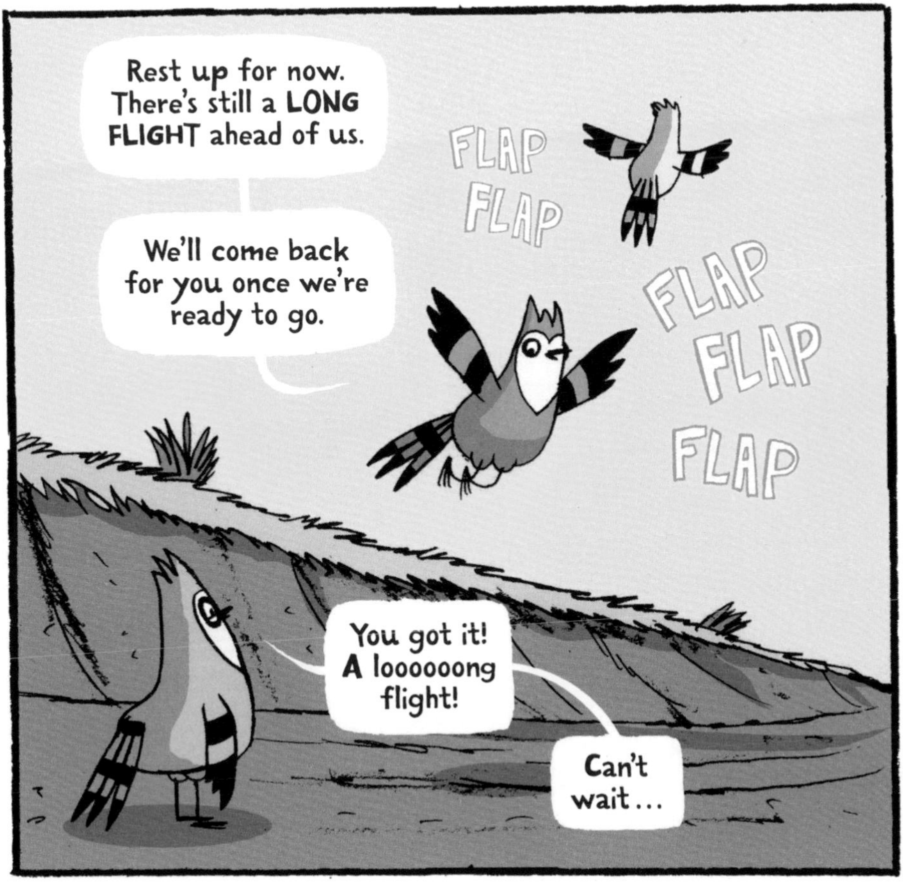
Rest up for now. There's still a LONG FLIGHT ahead of us.
We'll come back for you once we're ready to go.
FLAP
FLAP
FLAP
FLAP
FLAP
You got it! A loooooong flight!
Can't wait...

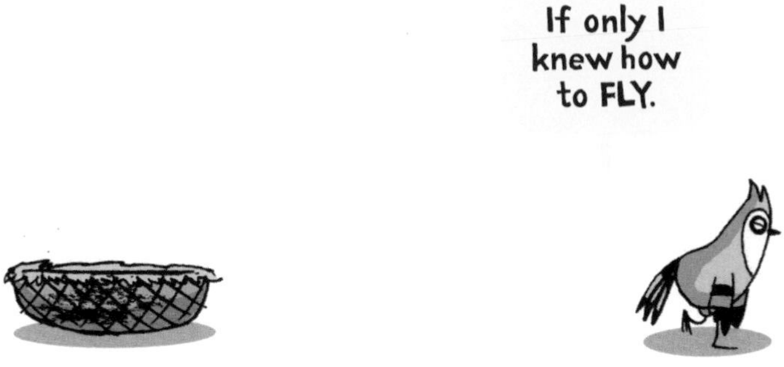
If only I knew how to FLY.

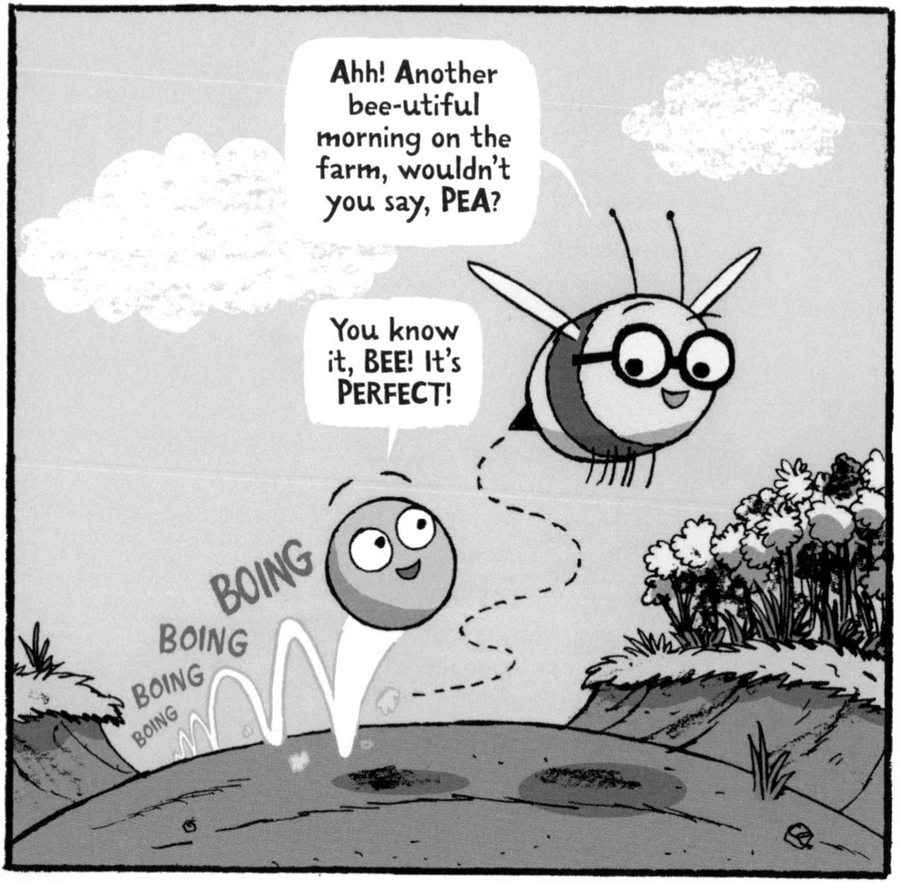
Ahh! Another bee-utiful morning on the farm, wouldn't you say, PEA?
You know it, BEE! It's PERFECT!
BOING
BOING
BOING
BOING

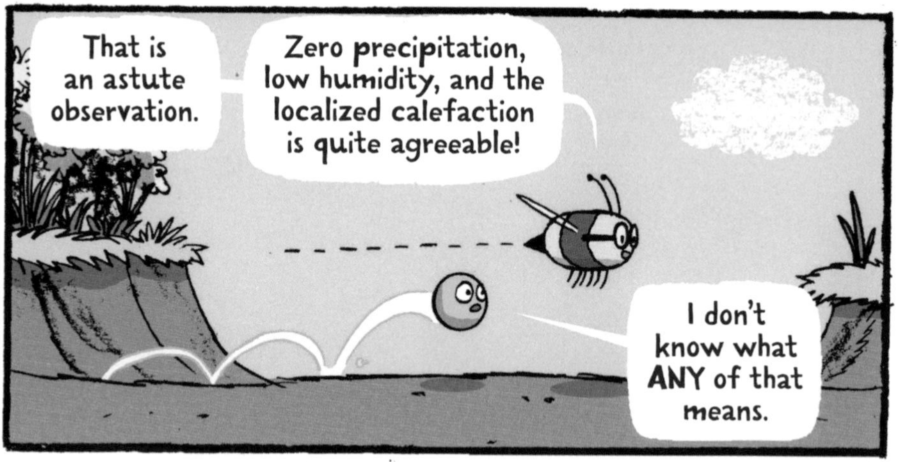
That is an astute observation.
Zero precipitation, low humidity, and the localized calefaction is quite agreeable!
I don't know what ANY of that means.

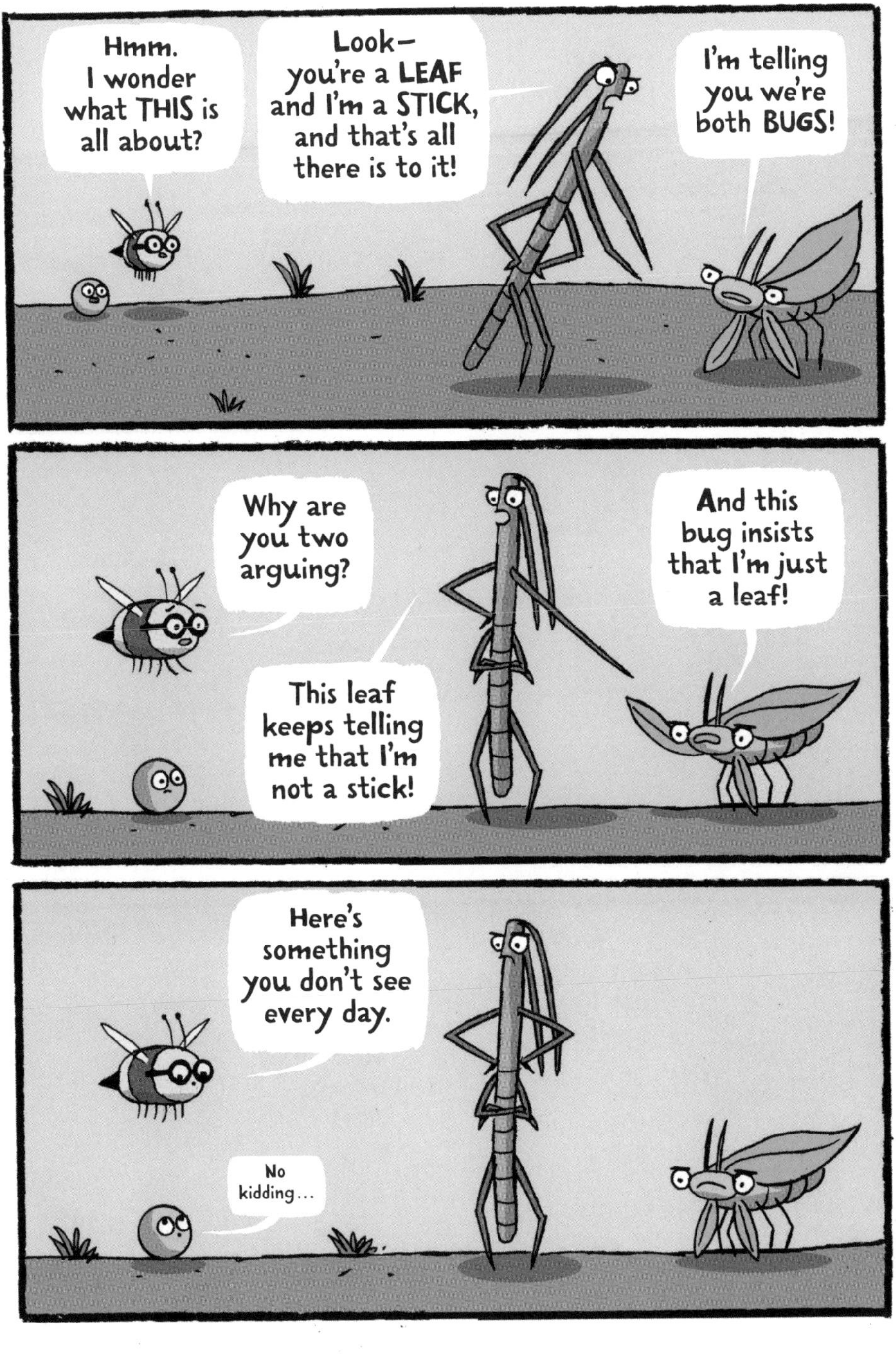
Hmm. I wonder what THIS is all about?
Look— you're a LEAF and I'm a STICK, and that's all there is to it!
I'm telling you we're both BUGS!
Why are you two arguing?
This leaf keeps telling me that I'm not a stick!
And this bug insists that I'm just a leaf!
Here's something you don't see every day.
No kidding...

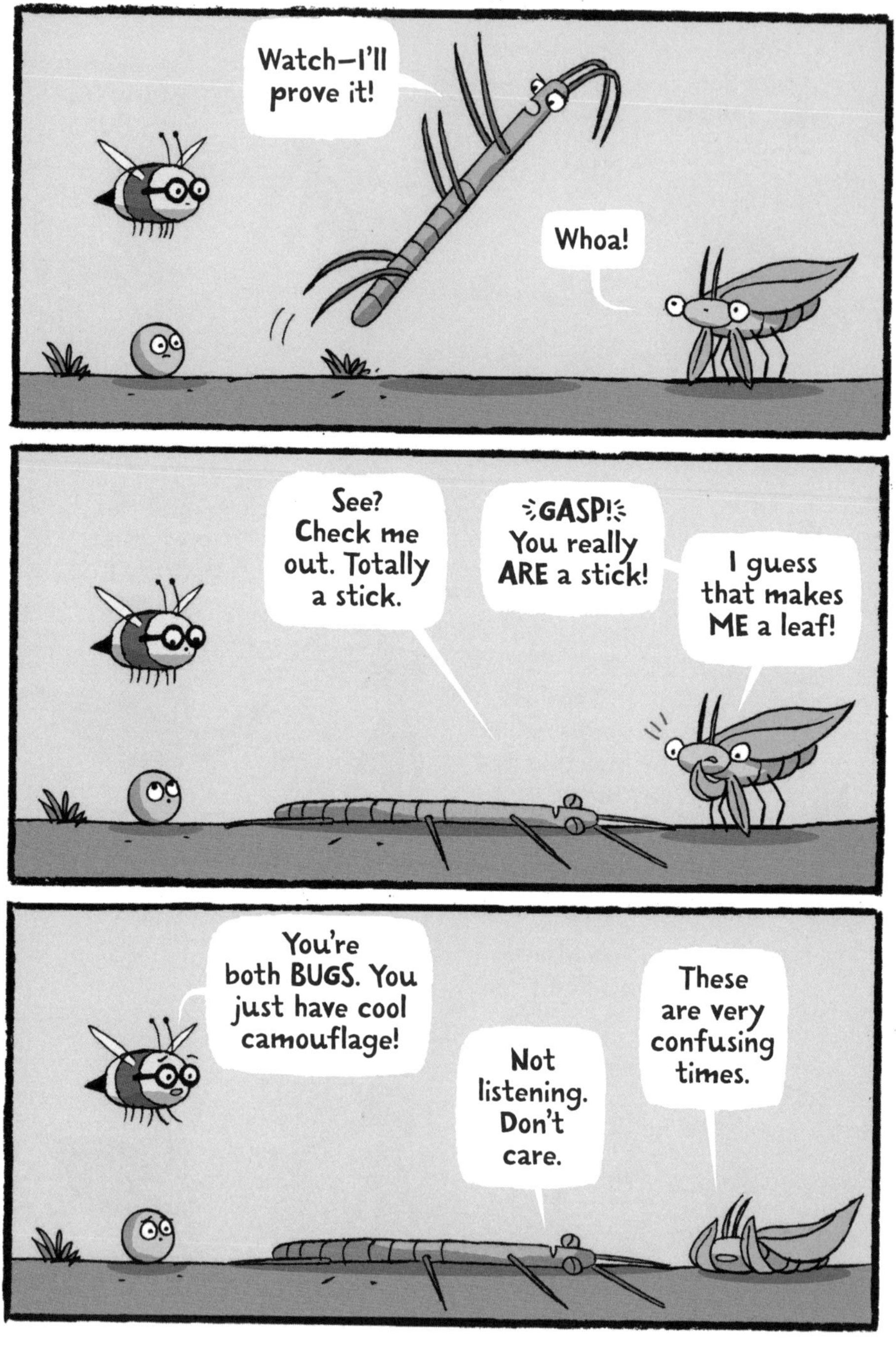
Watch—I'll prove it!
Whoa!
See? Check me out. Totally a stick.
GASP! You really ARE a stick!
I guess that makes ME a leaf!
You're both BUGS. You just have cool camouflage!
Not listening. Don't care.
These are very confusing times.

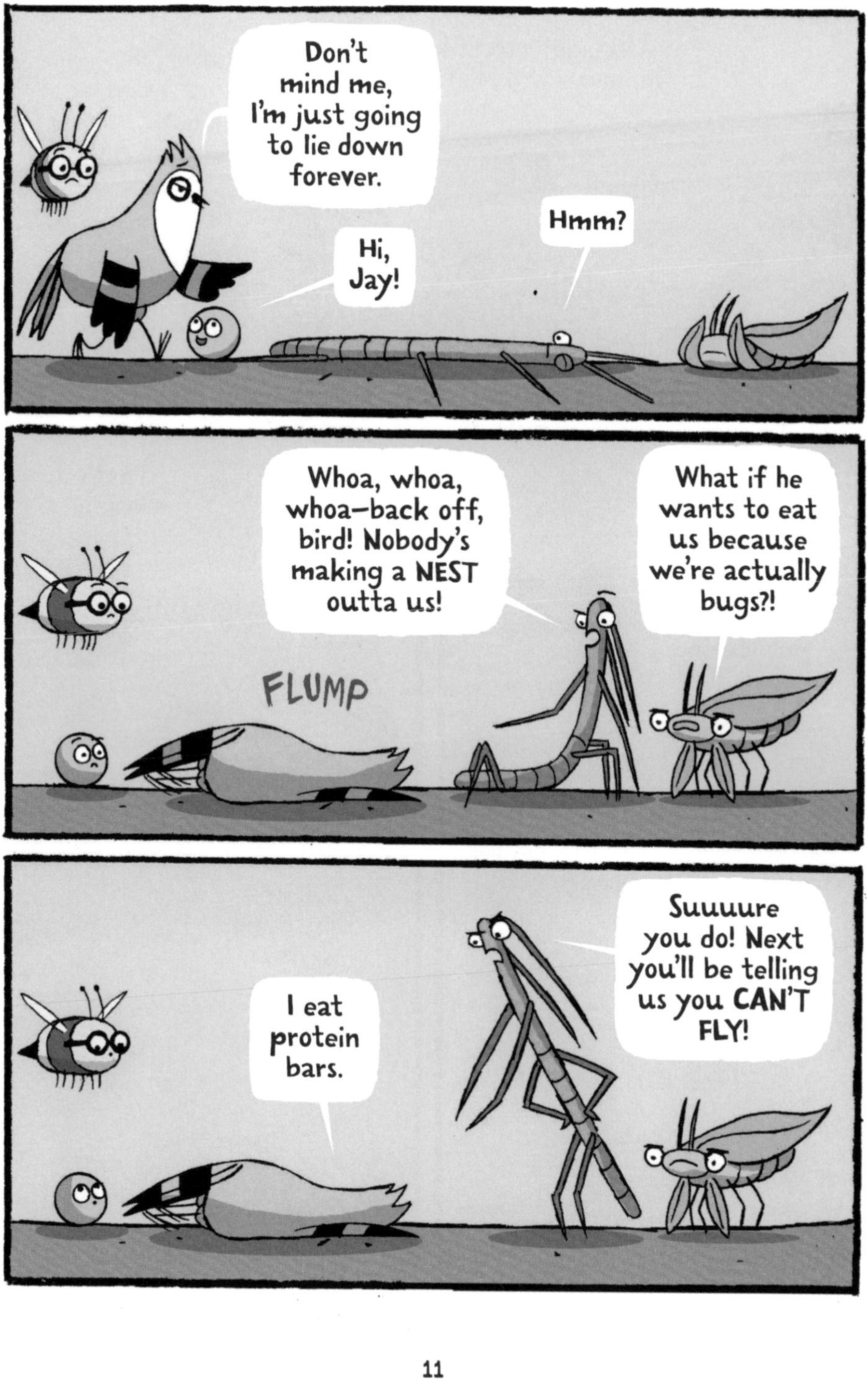
Don't mind me, I'm just going to lie down forever.
Hi, Jay!
Hmm?
Whoa, whoa, whoa—back off, bird! Nobody's making a NEST outta us!
What if he wants to eat us because we're actually bugs?!
FLUMP
I eat protein bars.
Suuuure you do! Next you'll be telling us you CAN'T FLY!

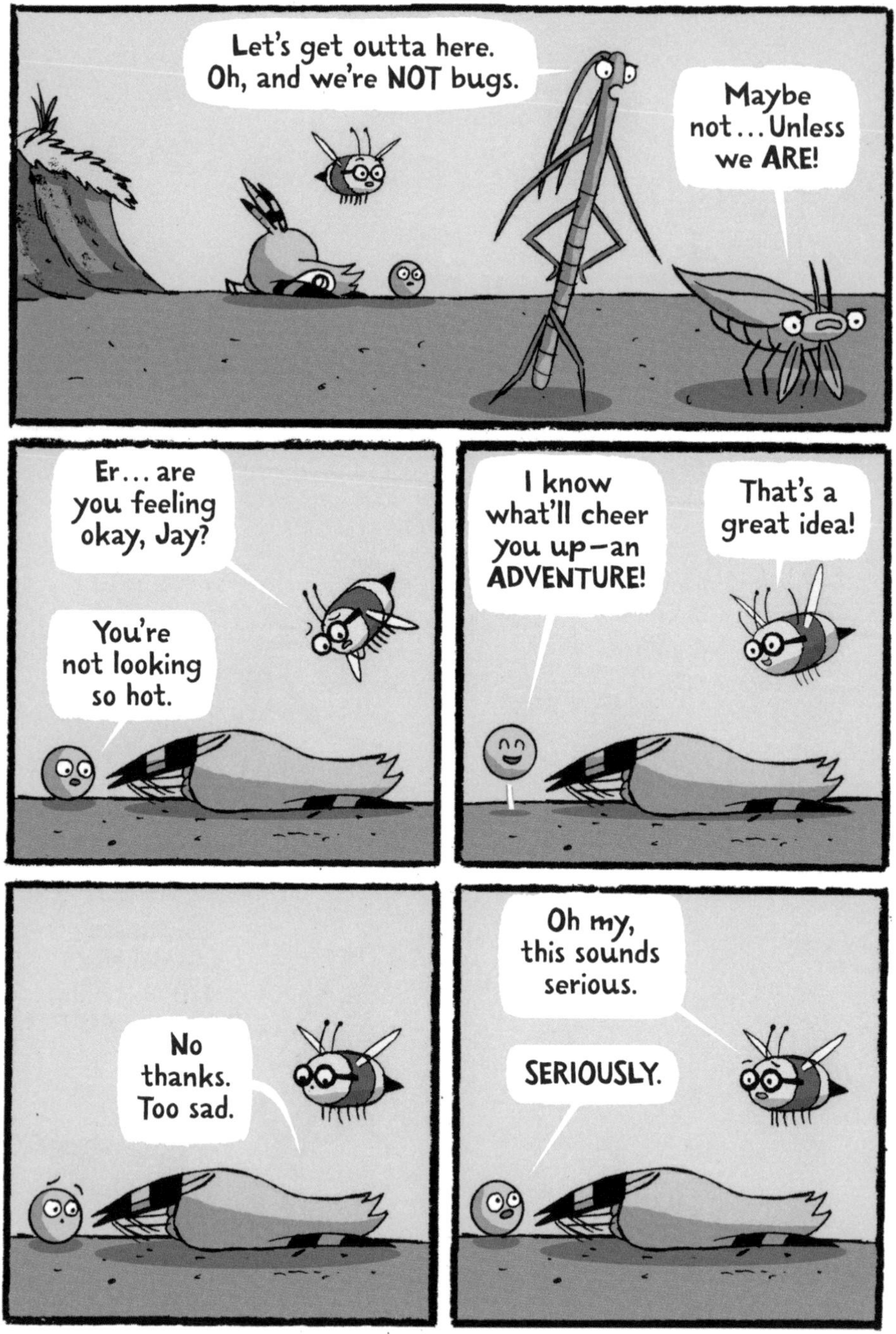
Let's get outta here.
Oh, and we're NOT bugs.
Maybe not... Unless we ARE!
Er... are you feeling okay, Jay?
You're not looking so hot.
I know what'll cheer you up—an ADVENTURE!
That's a great idea!
No thanks. Too sad.
Oh my, this sounds serious.
SERIOUSLY.

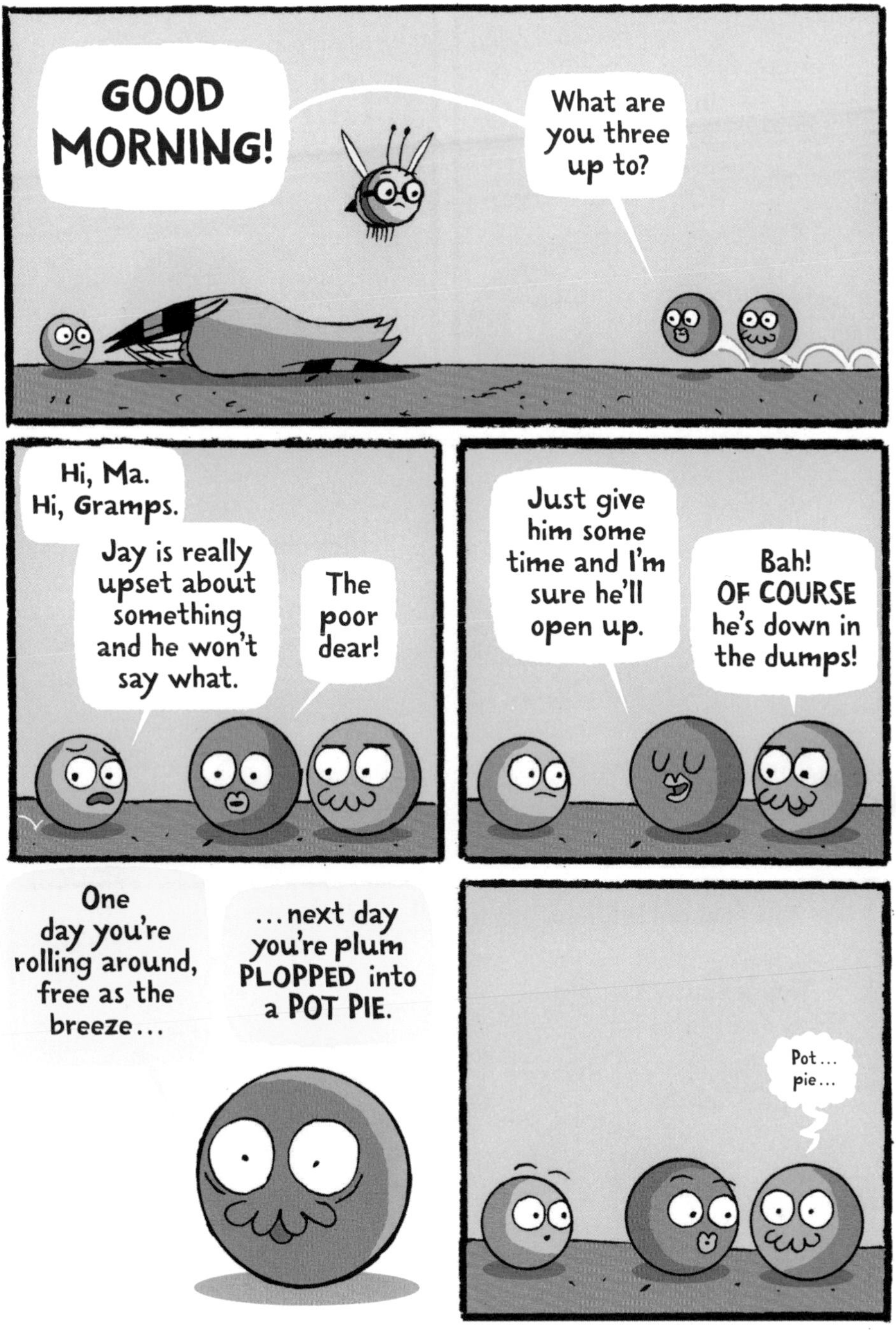
GOOD MORNING!
What are you three up to?
Hi, Ma. Hi, Gramps.
Jay is really upset about something and he won't say what.
The poor dear!
Just give him some time and I'm sure he'll open up.
Bah! OF COURSE he's down in the dumps!
One day you're rolling around, free as the breeze...
...next day you're plum PLOPPED into a POT PIE.
Pot... pie...

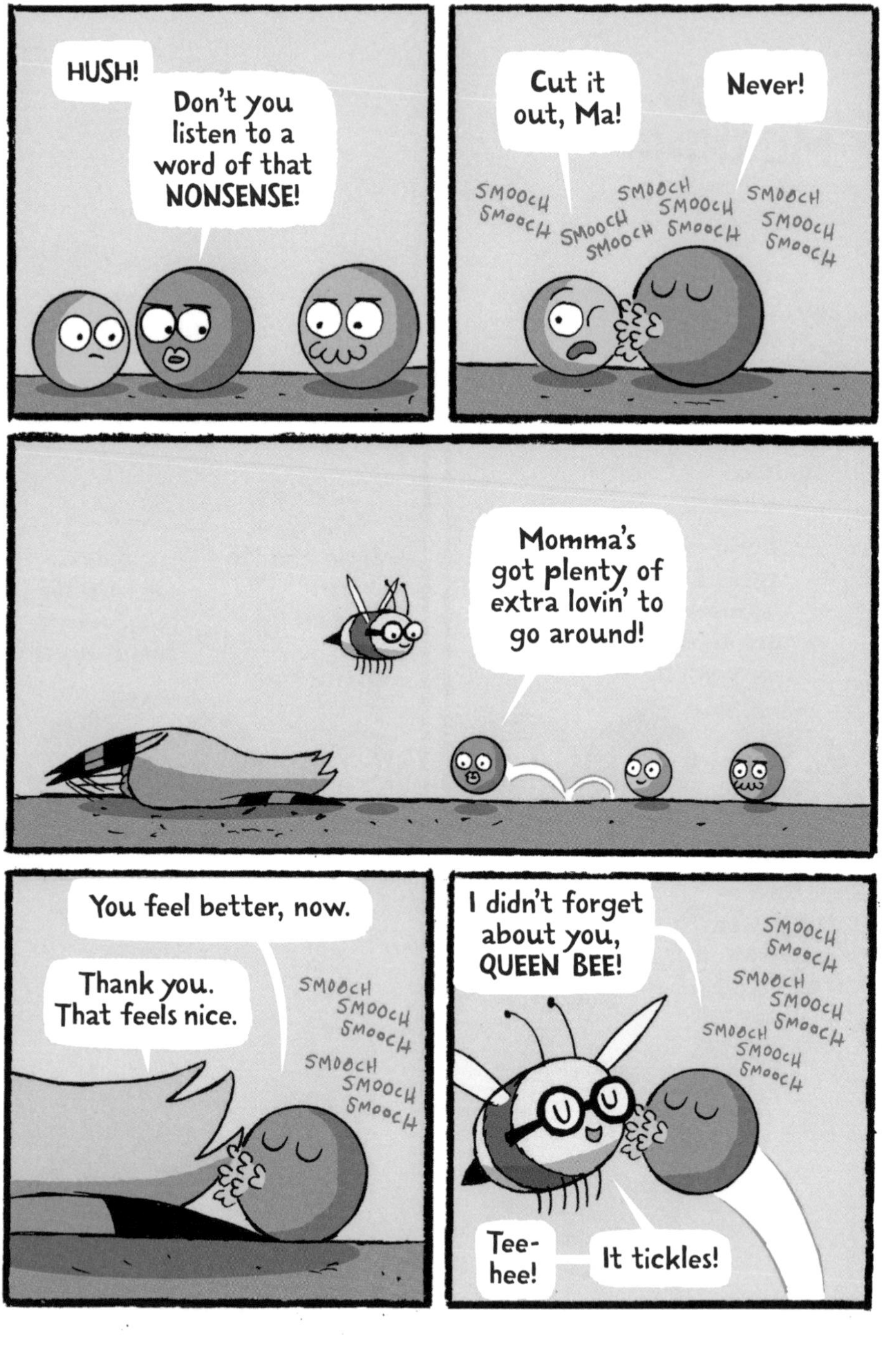
HUSH!
Don't you listen to a word of that NONSENSE!
Cut it out, Ma!
Never!
SMOOCH SMOOCH SMOOCH SMOOCH SMOOCH SMOOCH SMOOCH SMOOCH SMOOCH SMOOCH
Momma's got plenty of extra lovin' to go around!
You feel better, now.
Thank you. That feels nice.
SMOOCH SMOOCH SMOOCH SMOOCH SMOOCH SMOOCH
I didn't forget about you, QUEEN BEE!
SMOOCH SMOOCH SMOOCH SMOOCH SMOOCH SMOOCH SMOOCH SMOOCH
Tee-hee!
It tickles!

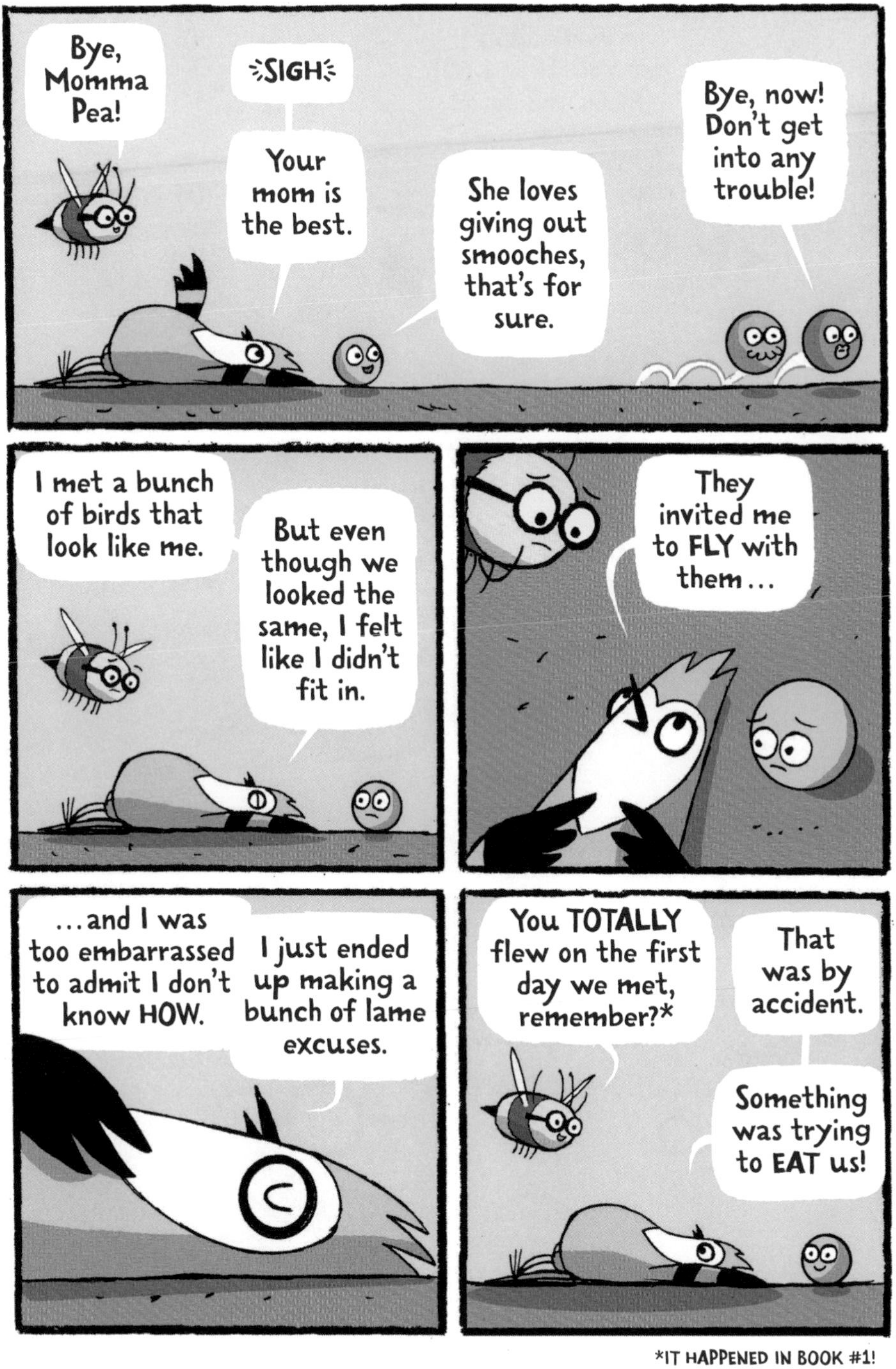
Bye, Momma Pea!
SIGH
Your mom is the best.
She loves giving out smooches, that's for sure.
Bye, now! Don't get into any trouble!
I met a bunch of birds that look like me.
But even though we looked the same, I felt like I didn't fit in.
They invited me to FLY with them...
...and I was too embarrassed to admit I don't know HOW.
I just ended up making a bunch of lame excuses.
You TOTALLY flew on the first day we met, remember?*
That was by accident.
Something was trying to EAT us!

*IT HAPPENED IN BOOK #1!

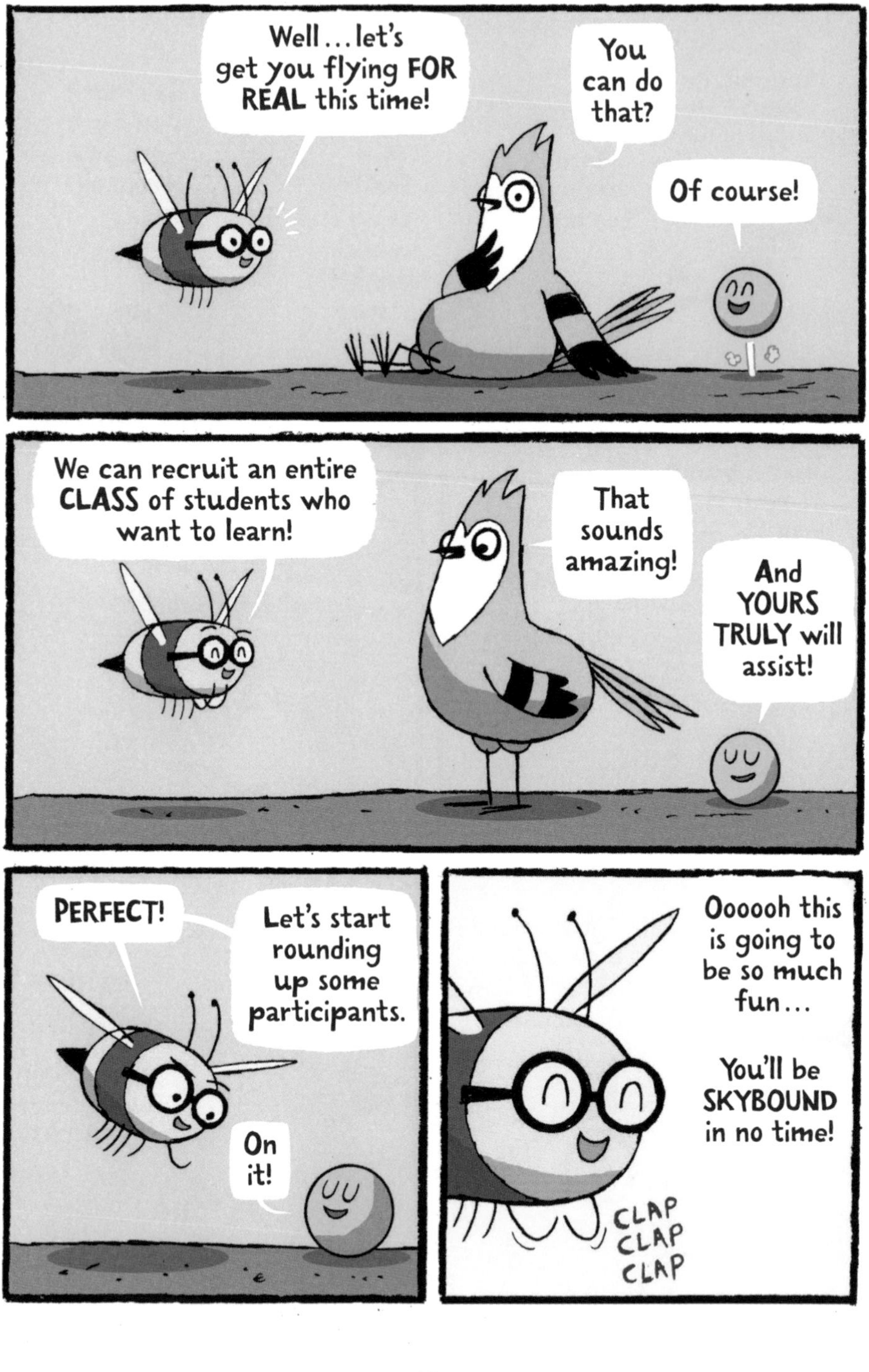
Well... let's get you flying FOR REAL this time!
You can do that?
Of course!
We can recruit an entire CLASS of students who want to learn!
That sounds amazing!
And YOURS TRULY will assist!
PERFECT!
Let's start rounding up some participants.
On it!
Oooooh this is going to be so much fun...
You'll be SKYBOUND in no time!
CLAP CLAP CLAP

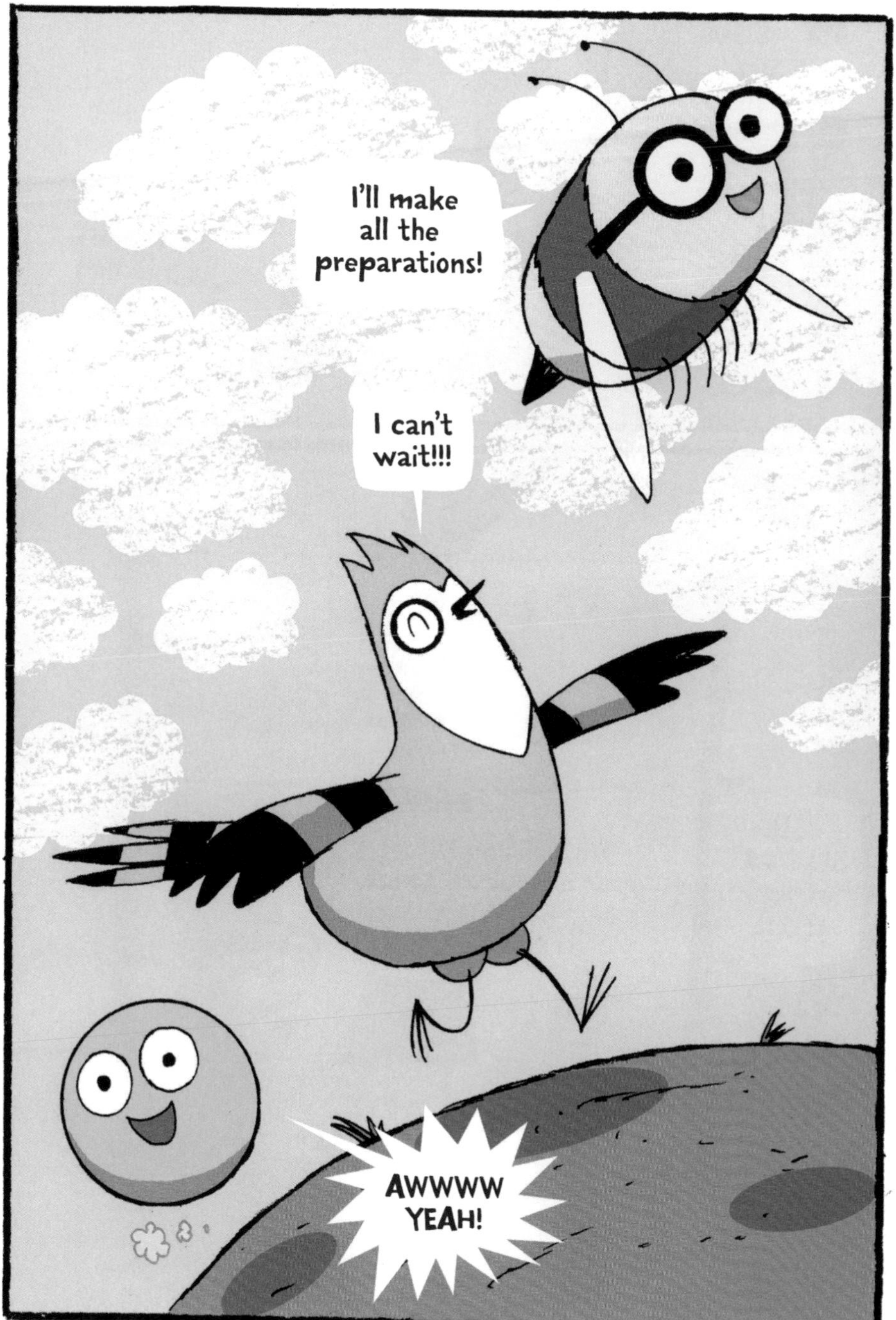
I'll make all the preparations!
I can't wait!!!
AWWWW YEAH!

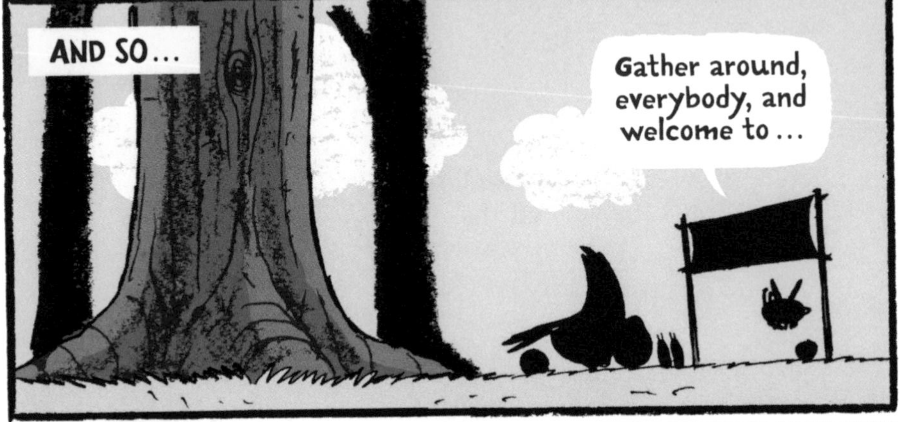
AND SO...
Gather around, everybody, and welcome to...

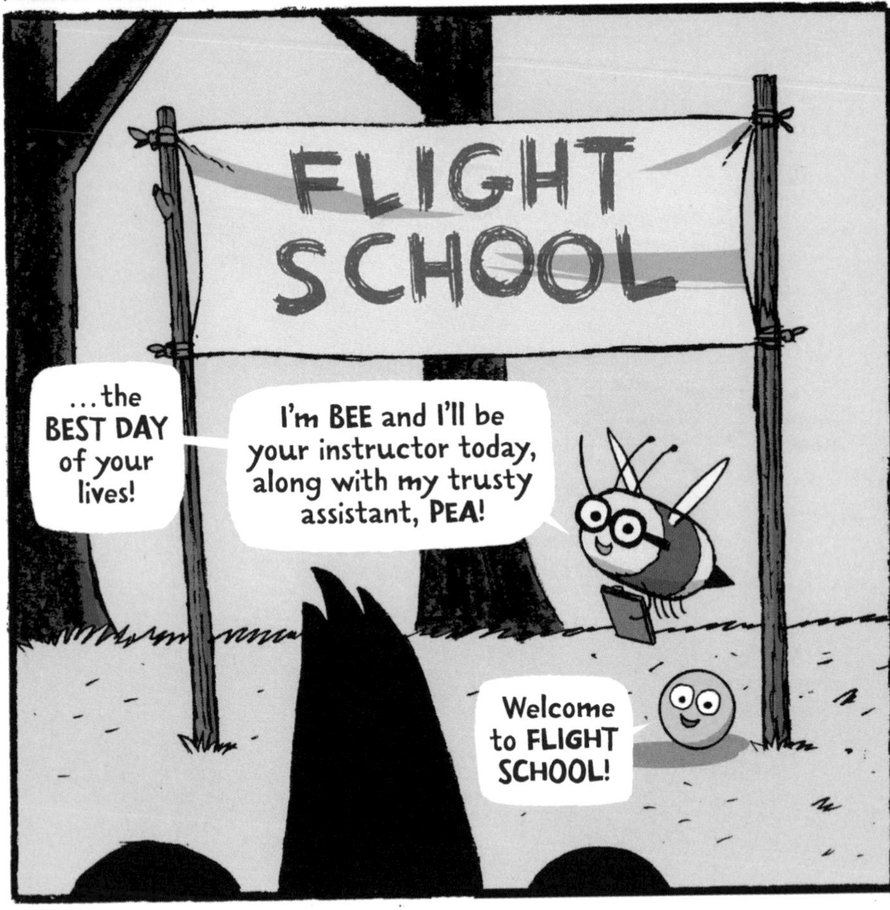
FLIGHT SCHOOL
...the BEST DAY of your lives!
I'm BEE and I'll be your instructor today, along with my trusty assistant, PEA!
Welcome to FLIGHT SCHOOL!

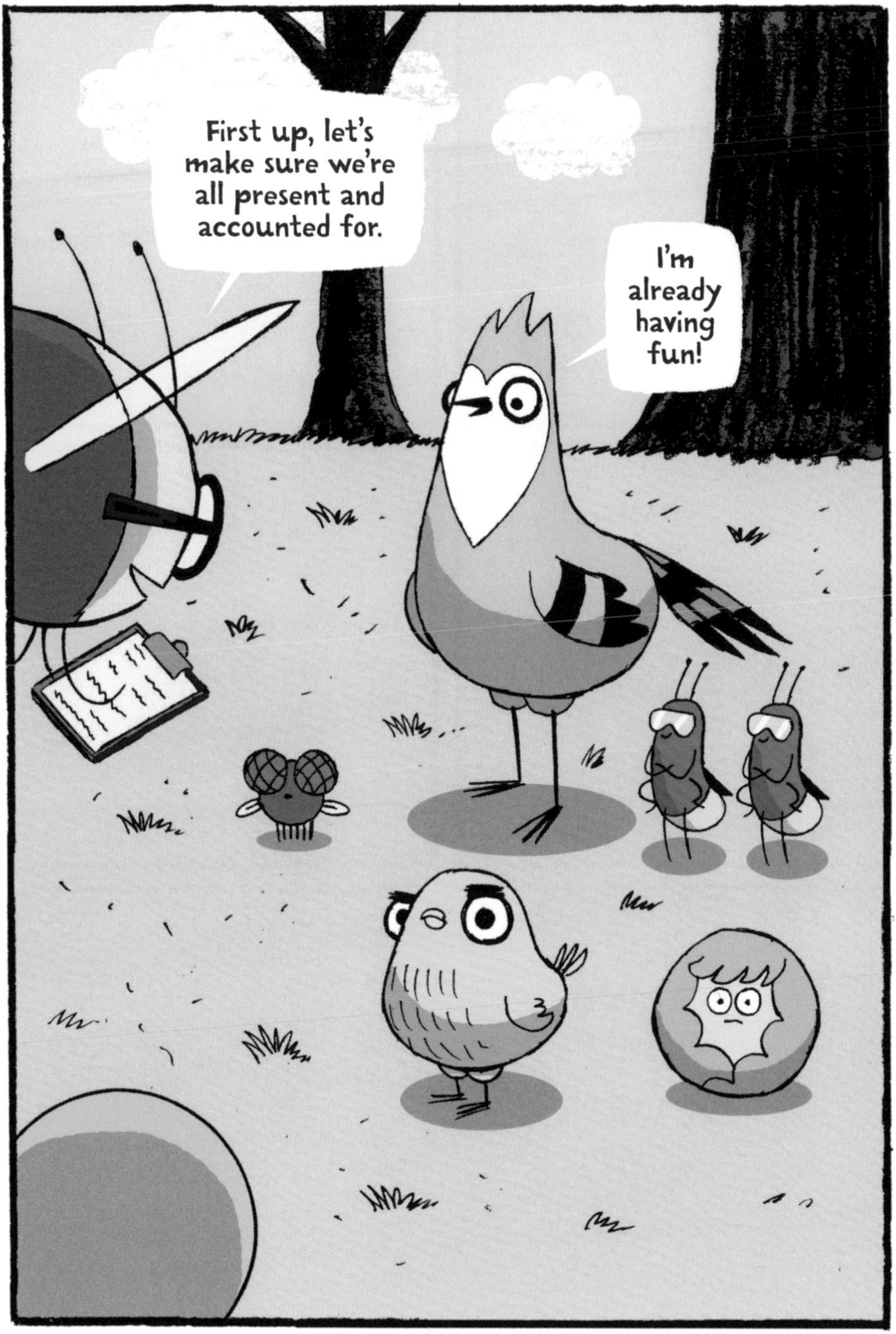
First up, let's make sure we're all present and accounted for.
I'm already having fun!

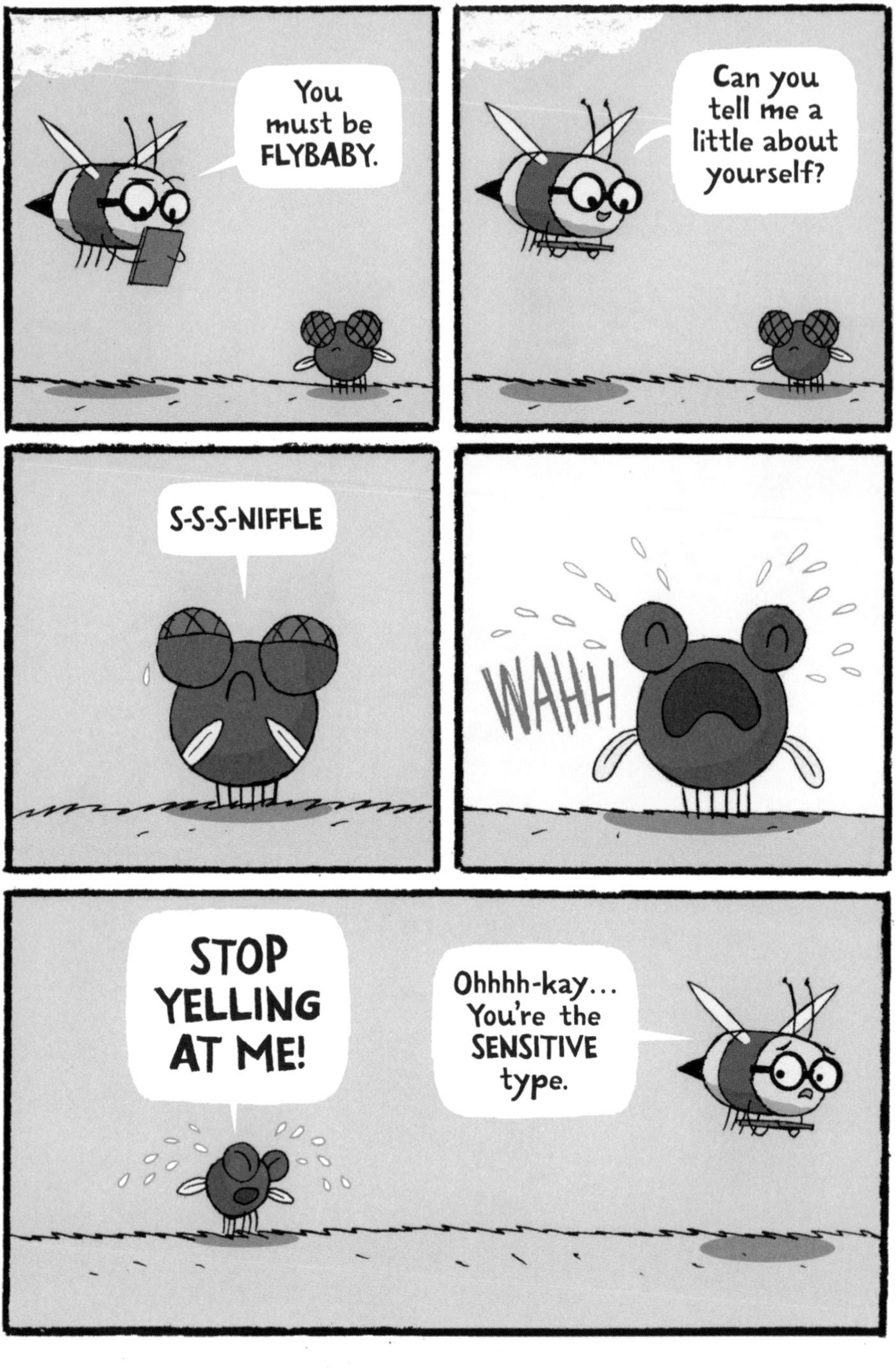
You must be FLYBABY.
Can you tell me a little about yourself?
S-S-S-NIFFLE
WAHH
STOP YELLING AT ME!
Ohhhh-kay... You're the SENSITIVE type.

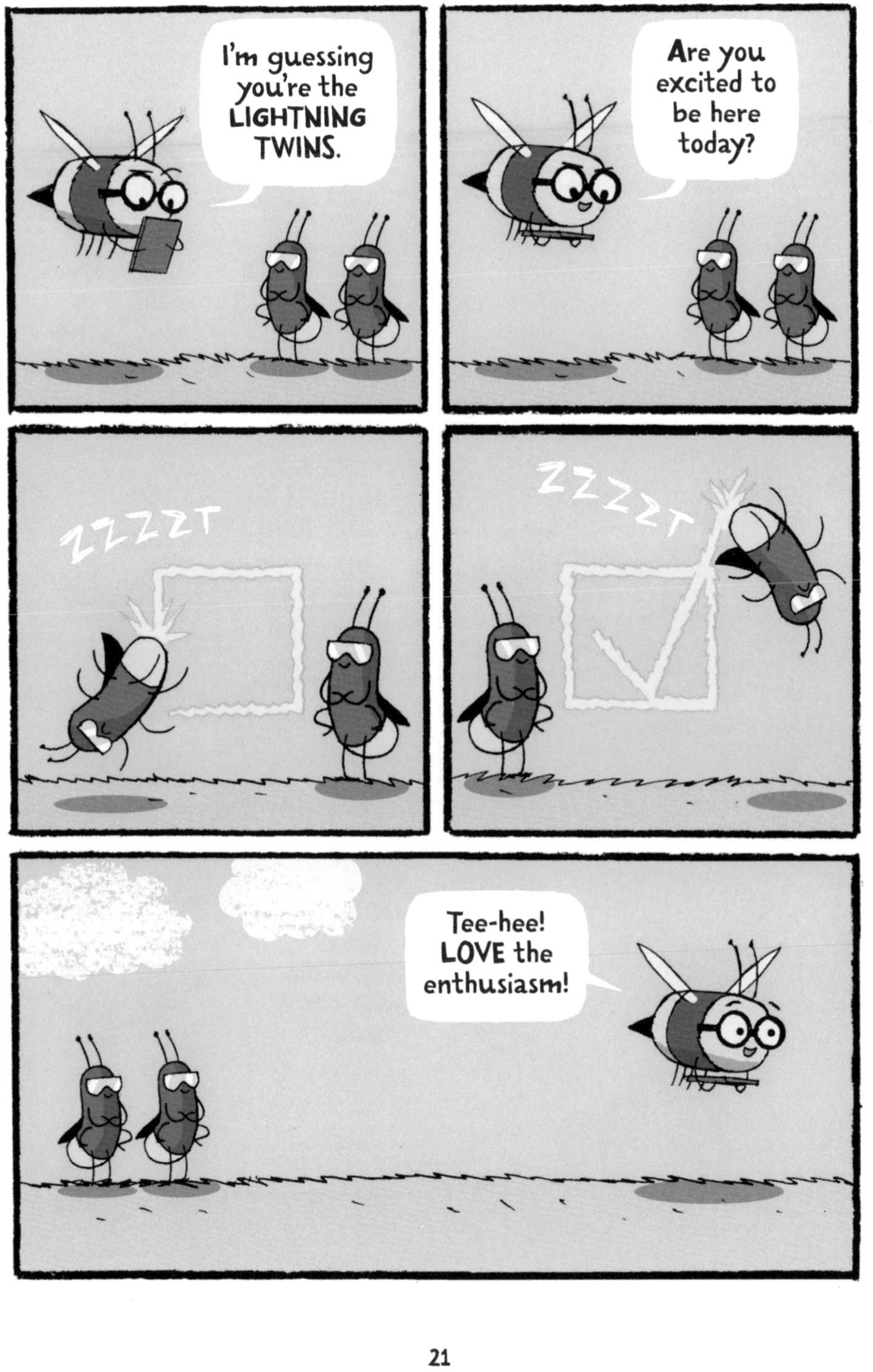
I'm guessing you're the LIGHTNING TWINS.
Are you excited to be here today?
ZZZZT
ZZZZT
Tee-hee! LOVE the enthusiasm!

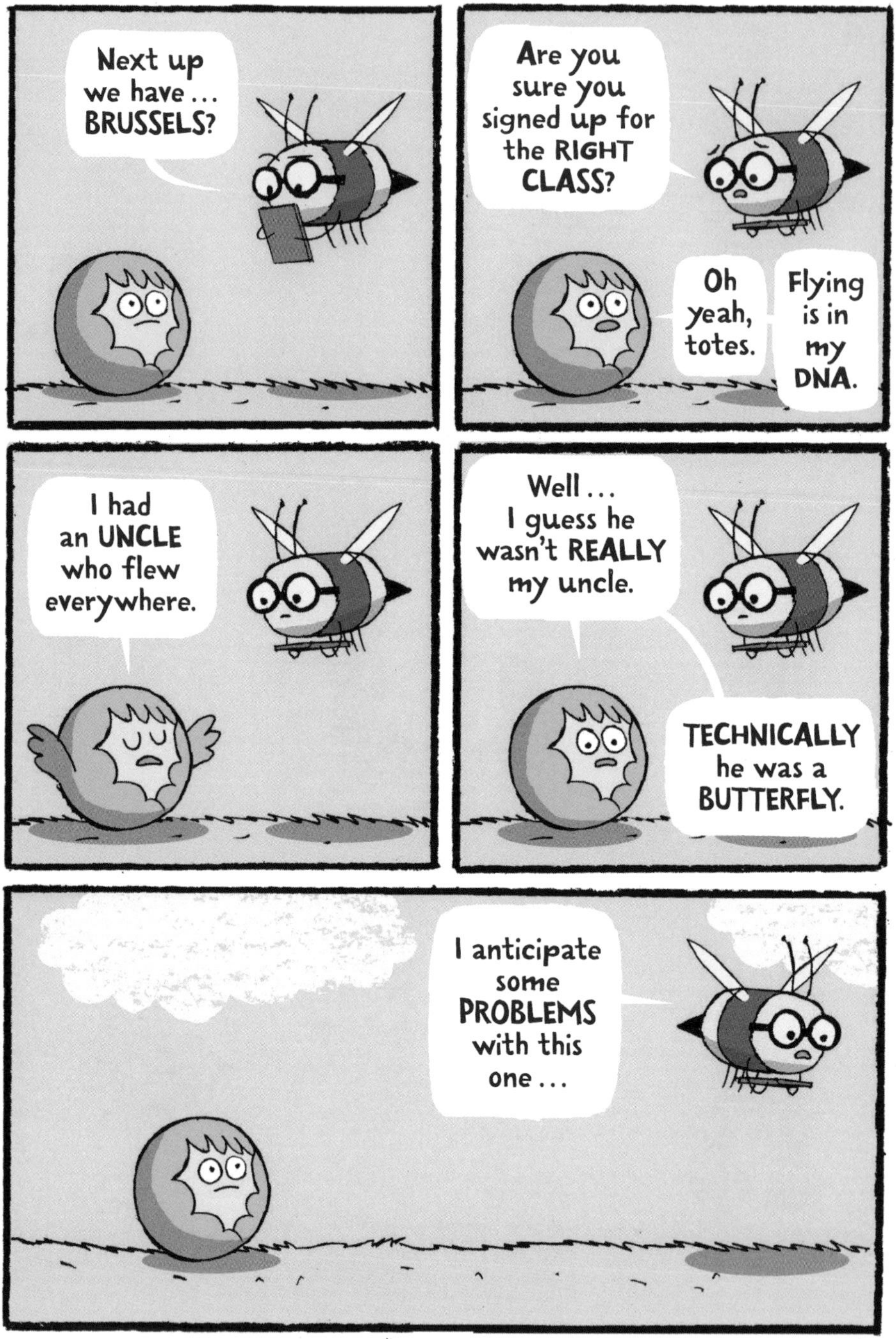
Next up we have ... BRUSSELS?
Are you sure you signed up for the RIGHT CLASS?
Oh yeah, totes.
Flying is in my DNA.
I had an UNCLE who flew everywhere.
Well ... I guess he wasn't REALLY my uncle.
TECHNICALLY he was a BUTTERFLY.
I anticipate some PROBLEMS with this one ...

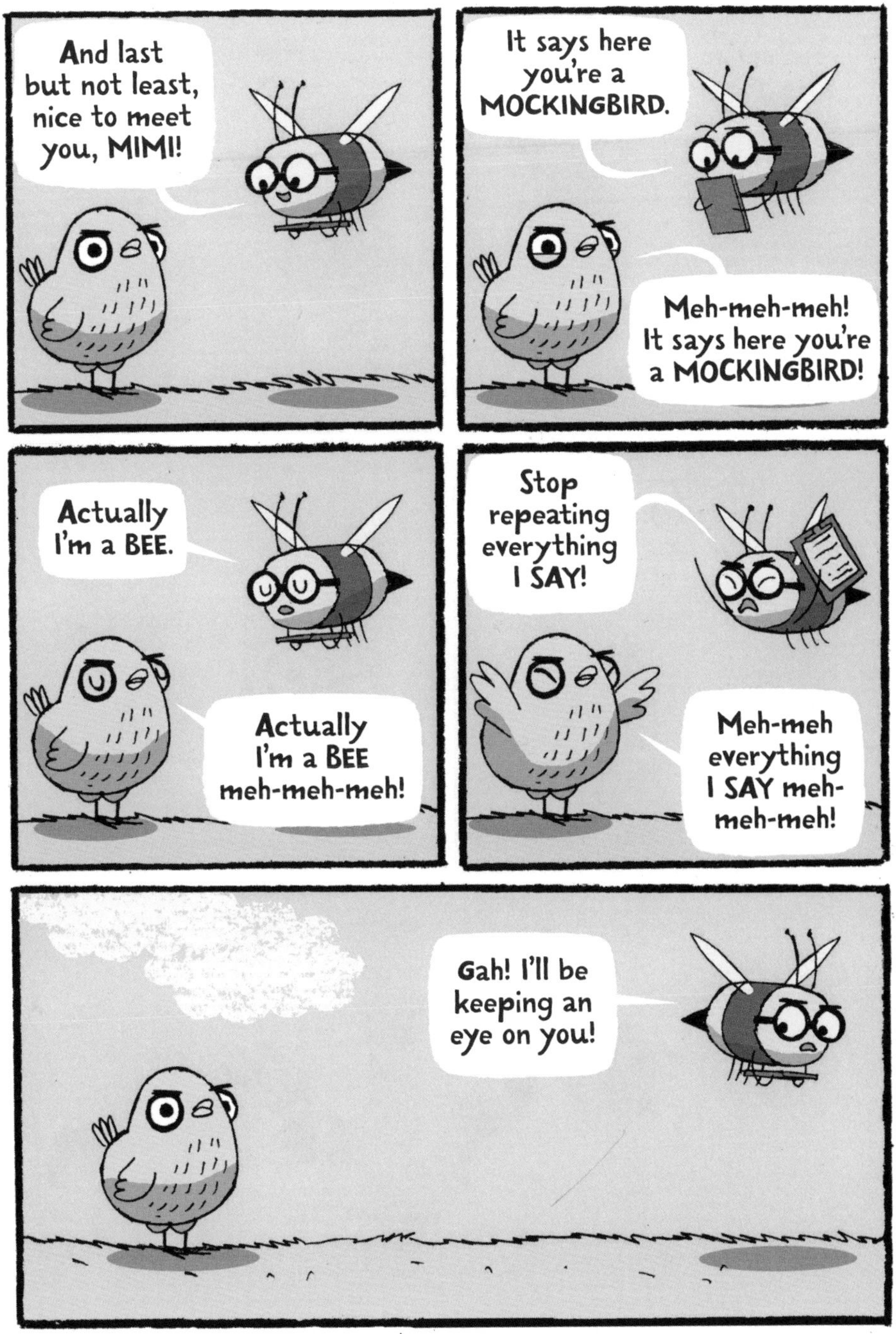
And last but not least, nice to meet you, MIMI!
It says here you're a MOCKINGBIRD.
Meh-meh-meh! It says here you're a MOCKINGBIRD!
Actually I'm a BEE.
Actually I'm a BEE meh-meh-meh!
Stop repeating everything I SAY!
Meh-meh everything I SAY meh-meh-meh!
Gah! I'll be keeping an eye on you!

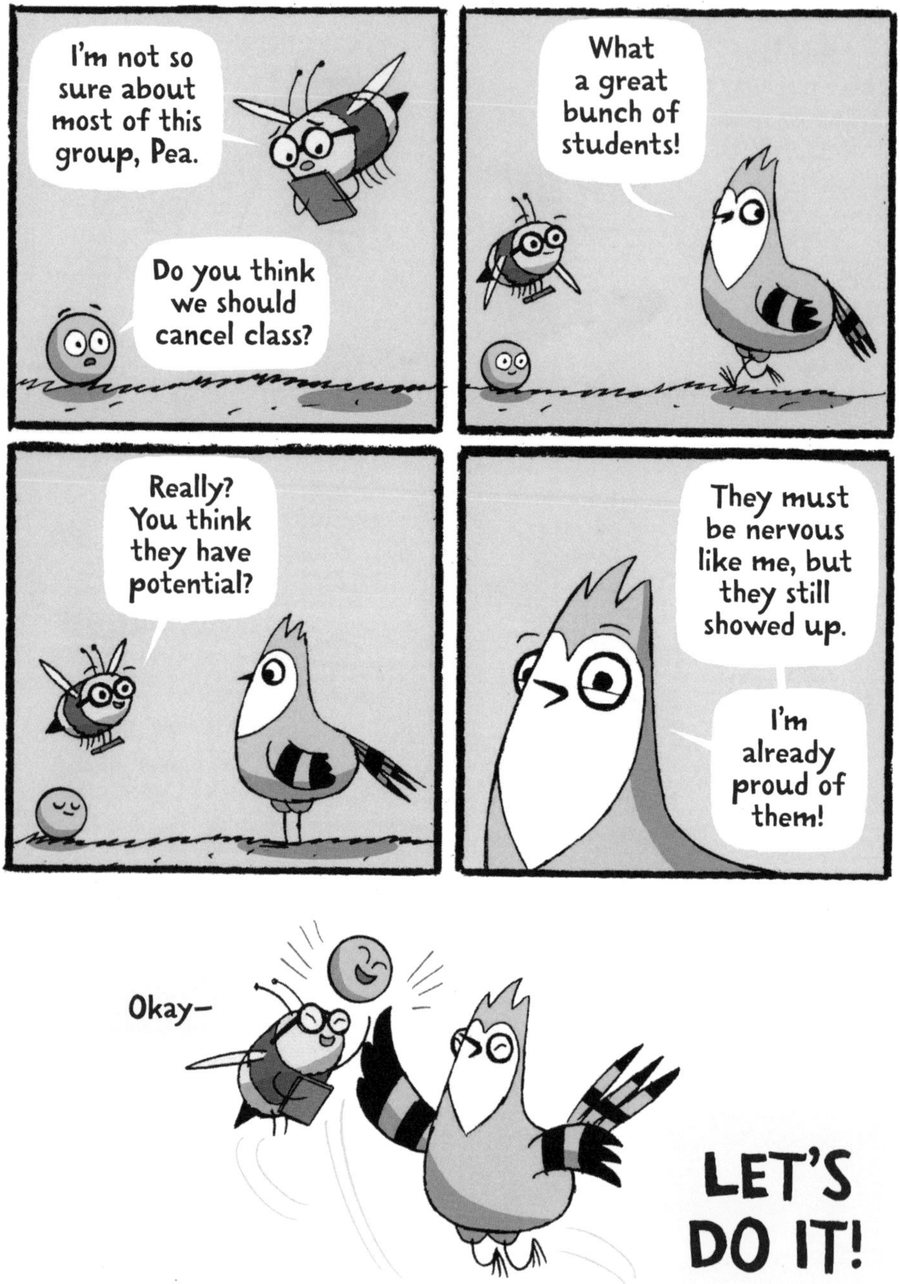
I'm not so sure about most of this group, Pea.
Do you think we should cancel class?
What a great bunch of students!
Really? You think they have potential?
They must be nervous like me, but they still showed up.
I'm already proud of them!
Okay–
LET'S DO IT!

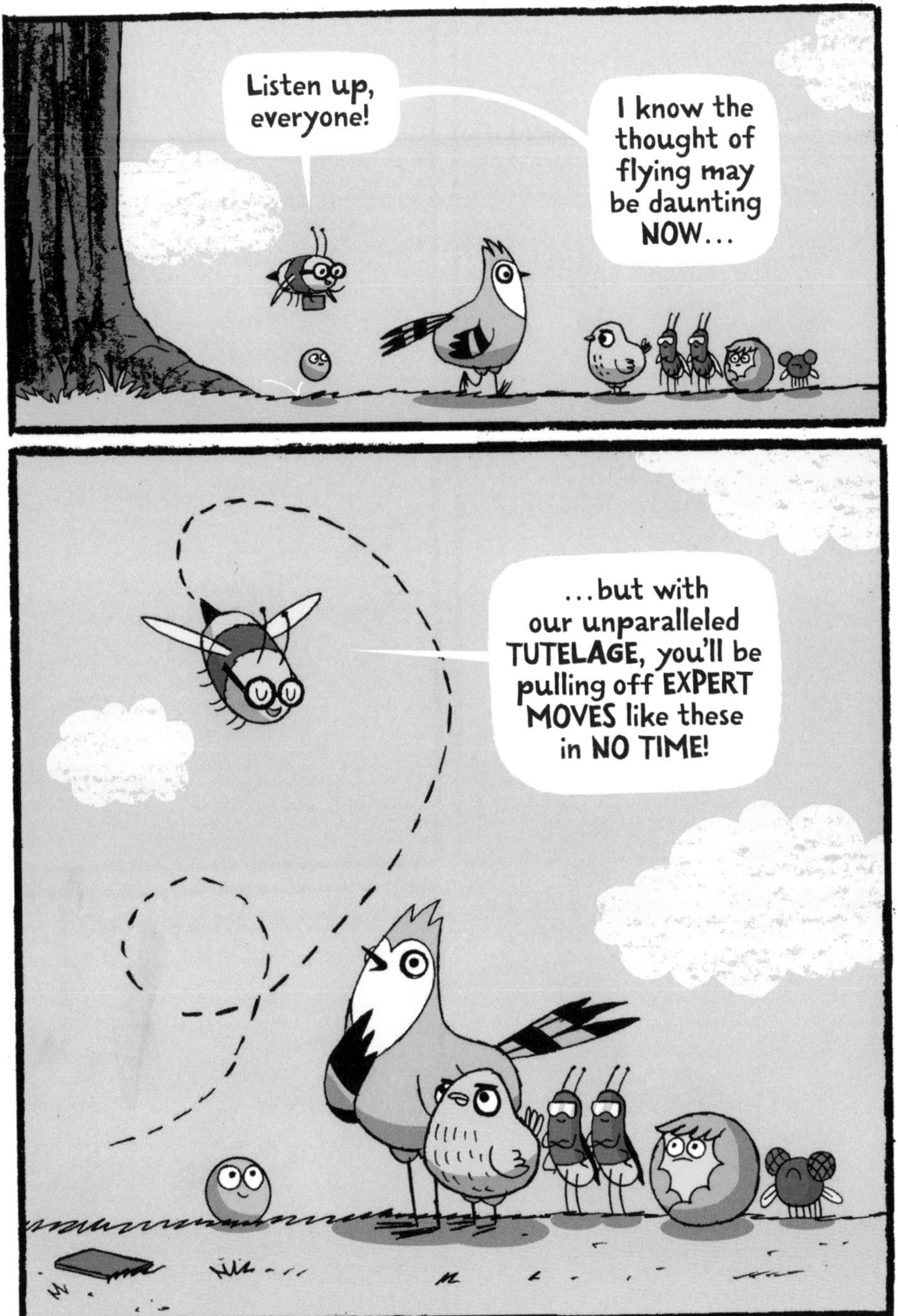
Listen up, everyone!
I know the thought of flying may be daunting NOW...
...but with our unparalleled TUTELAGE, you'll be pulling off EXPERT MOVES like these in NO TIME!

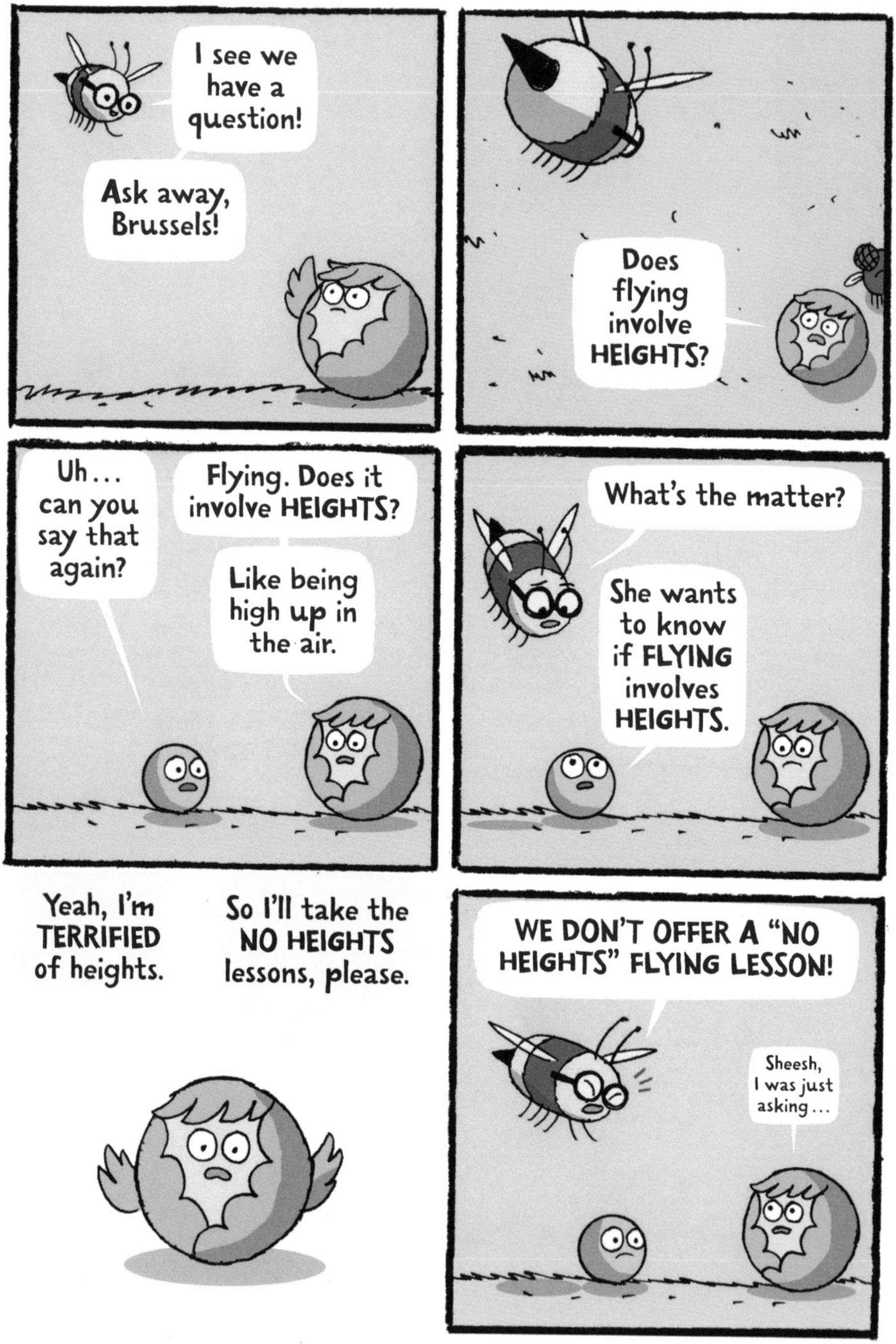
I see we have a question!
Ask away, Brussels!
Does flying involve HEIGHTS?
Uh... can you say that again?
Flying. Does it involve HEIGHTS?
Like being high up in the air.
What's the matter?
She wants to know if FLYING involves HEIGHTS.
Yeah, I'm TERRIFIED of heights.
So I'll take the NO HEIGHTS lessons, please.
WE DON'T OFFER A "NO HEIGHTS" FLYING LESSON!
Sheesh, I was just asking...

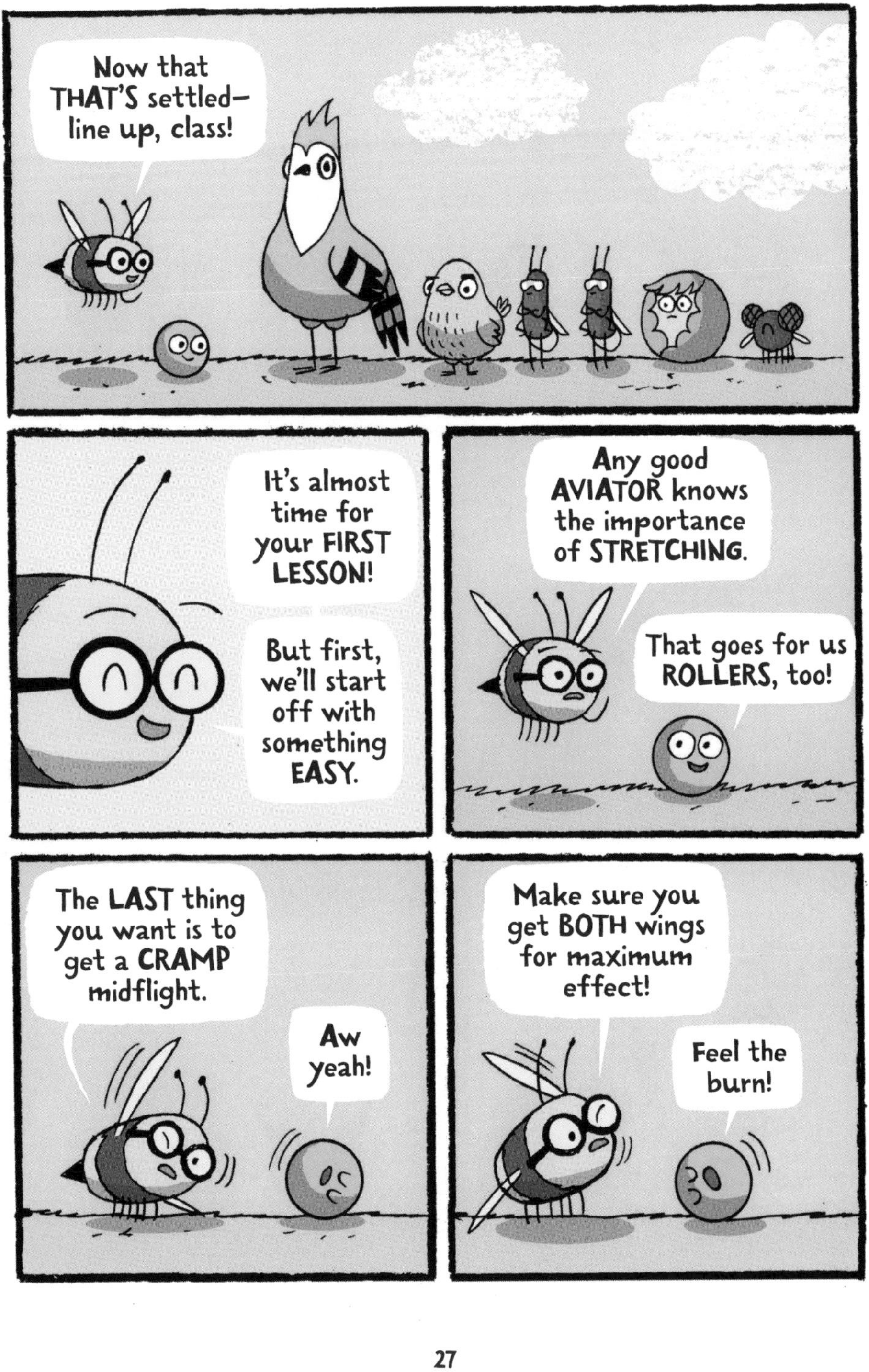
Now that THAT'S settled—line up, class!
It's almost time for your FIRST LESSON!
But first, we'll start off with something EASY.
Any good AVIATOR knows the importance of STRETCHING.
That goes for us ROLLERS, too!
The LAST thing you want is to get a CRAMP midflight.
Aw yeah!
Make sure you get BOTH wings for maximum effect!
Feel the burn!

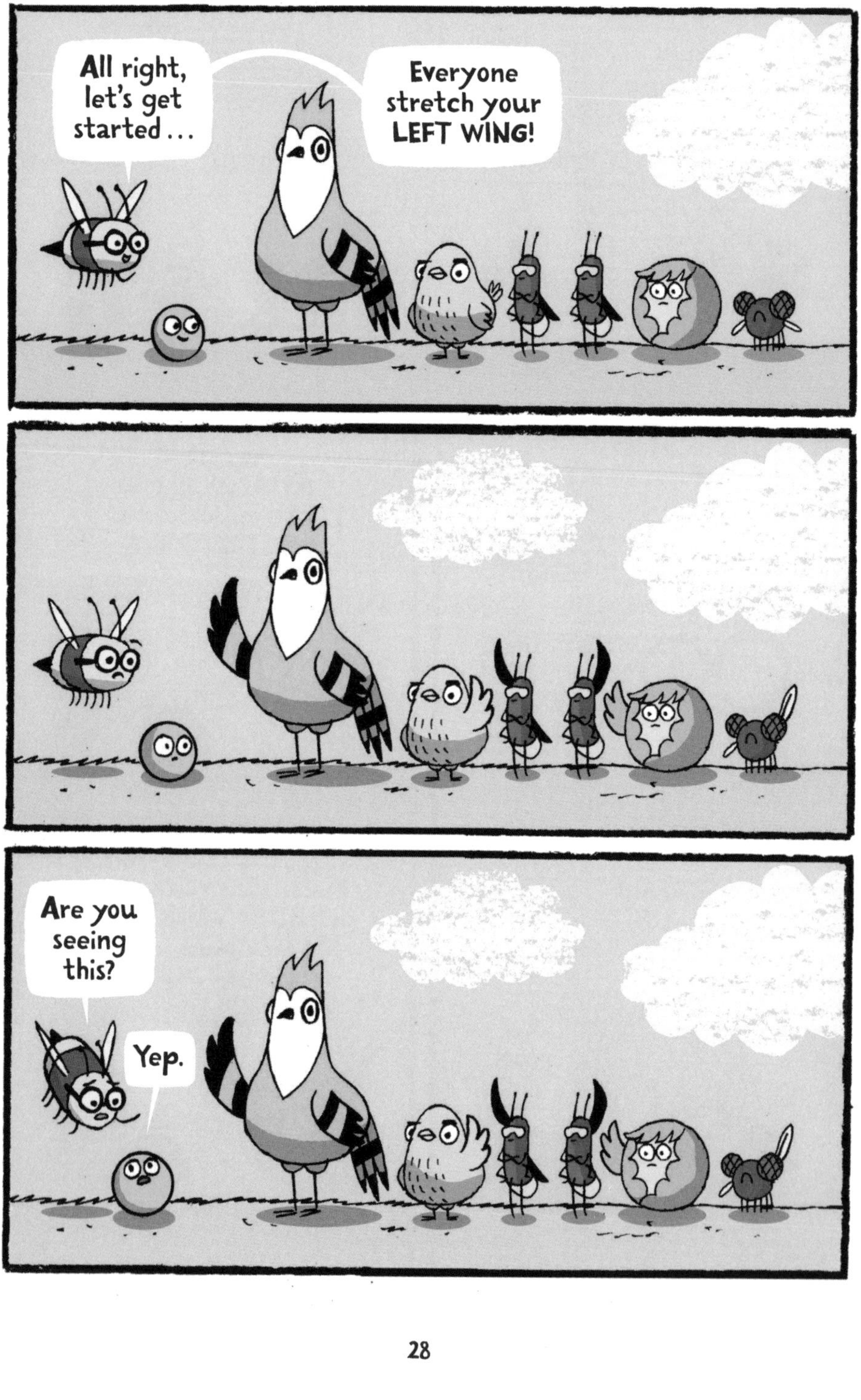
All right, let's get started . . .
Everyone stretch your LEFT WING!
Are you seeing this?
Yep.

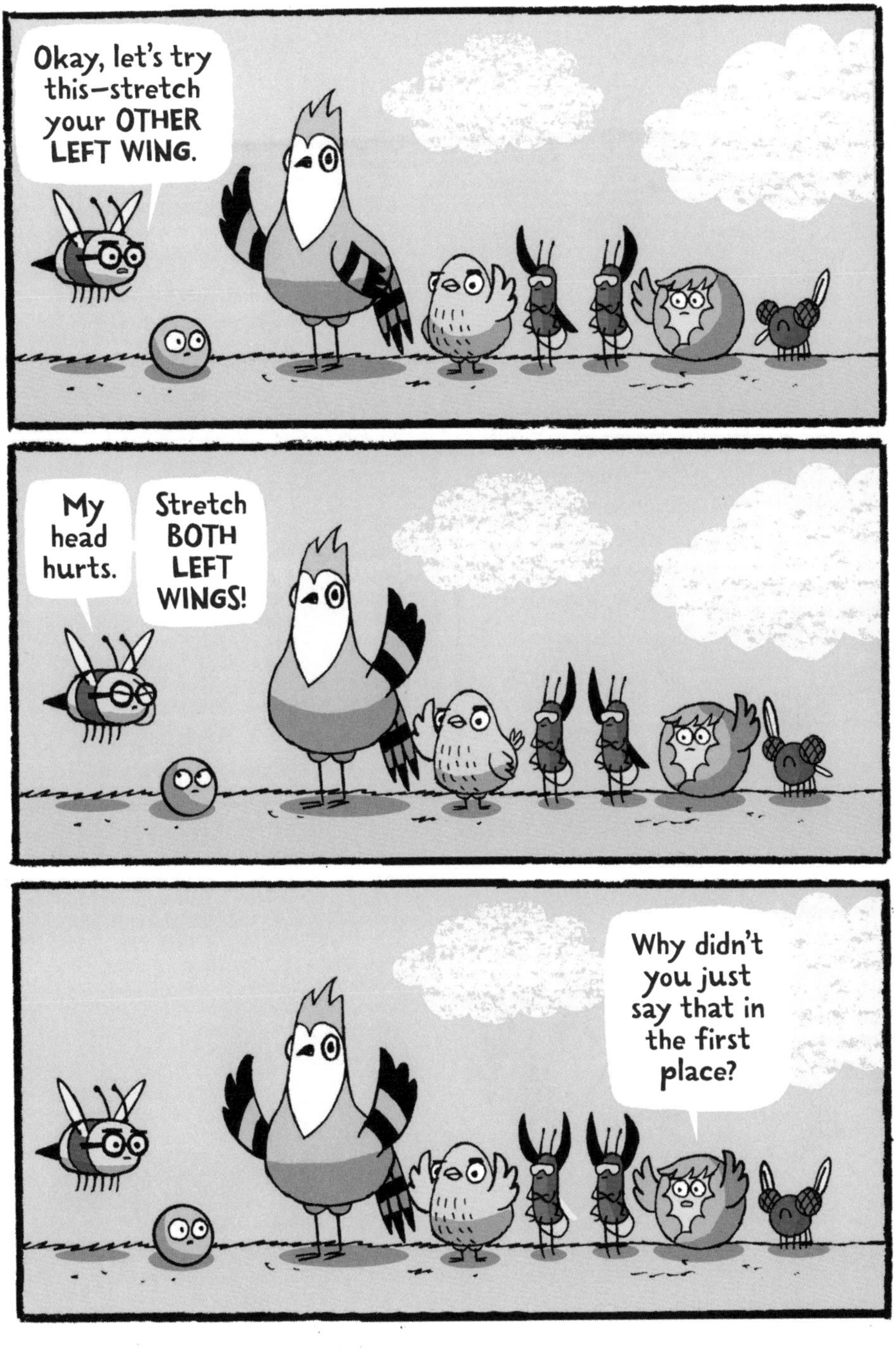
Okay, let's try this—stretch your OTHER LEFT WING.
My head hurts.
Stretch BOTH LEFT WINGS!
Why didn't you just say that in the first place?

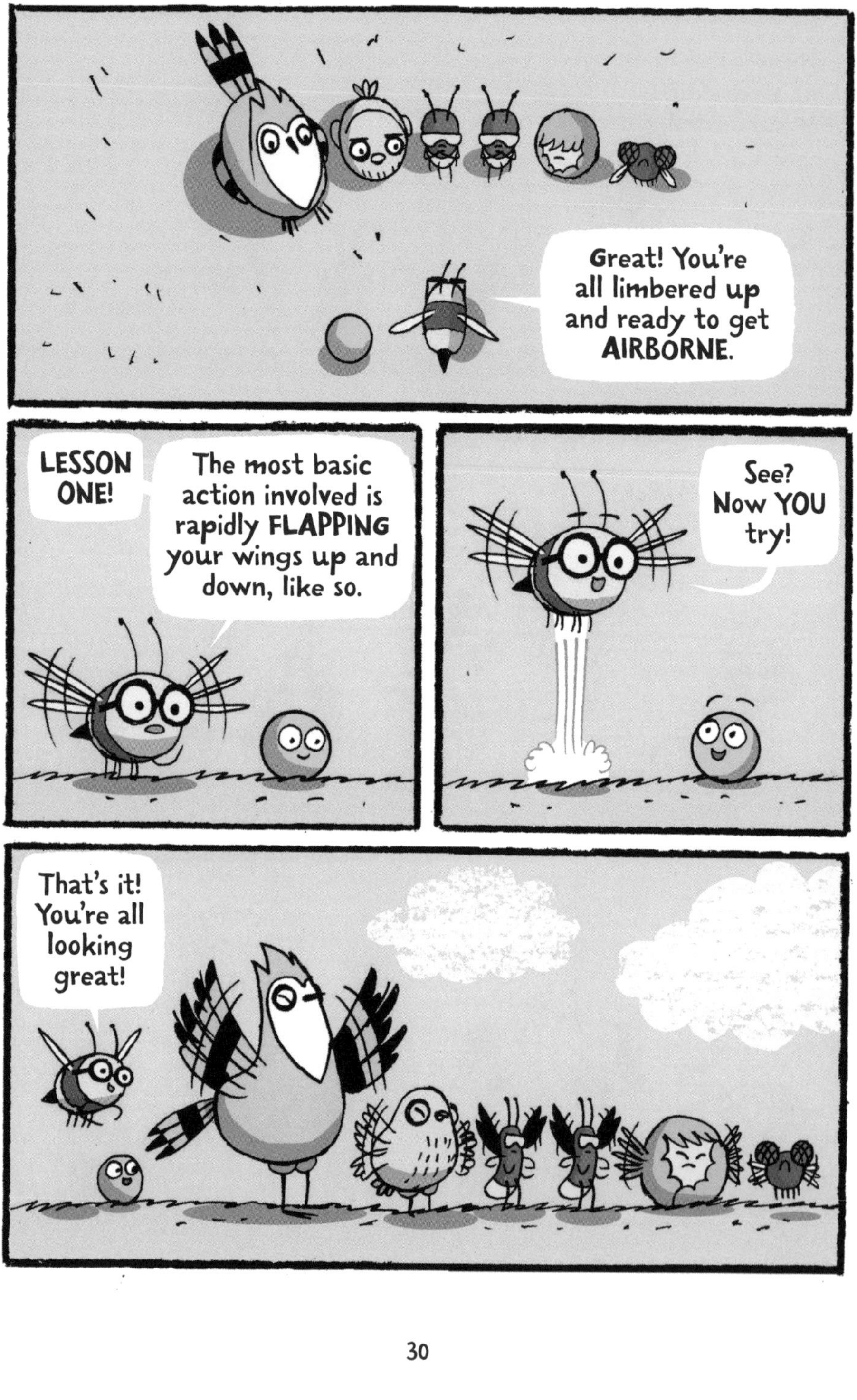
Great! You're all limbered up and ready to get AIRBORNE.
LESSON ONE!
The most basic action involved is rapidly FLAPPING your wings up and down, like so.
See? Now YOU try!
That's it! You're all looking great!

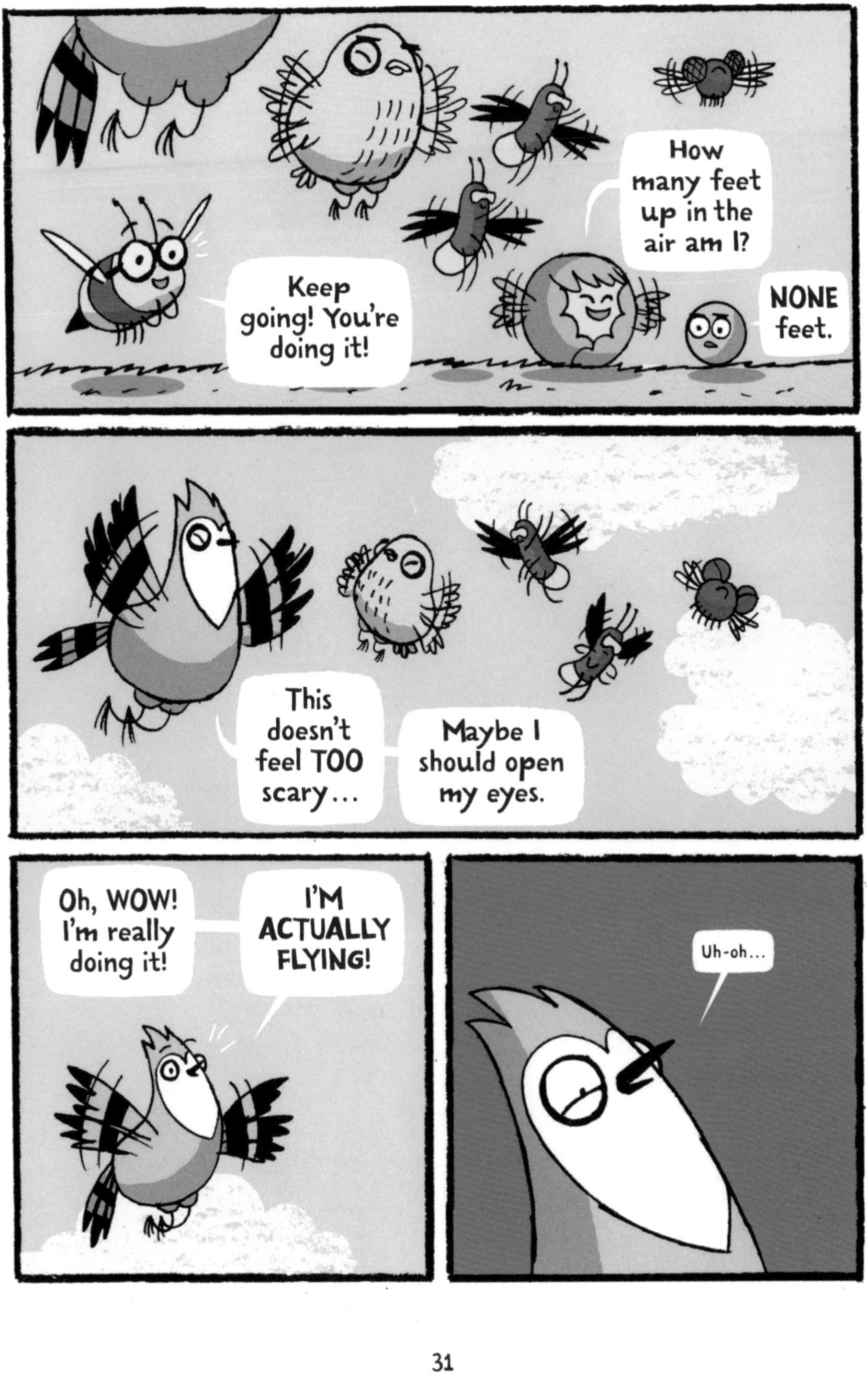
How many feet up in the air am I?
Keep going! You're doing it!
NONE feet.
This doesn't feel TOO scary…
Maybe I should open my eyes.
Oh, WOW! I'm really doing it!
I'M ACTUALLY FLYING!
Uh-oh…

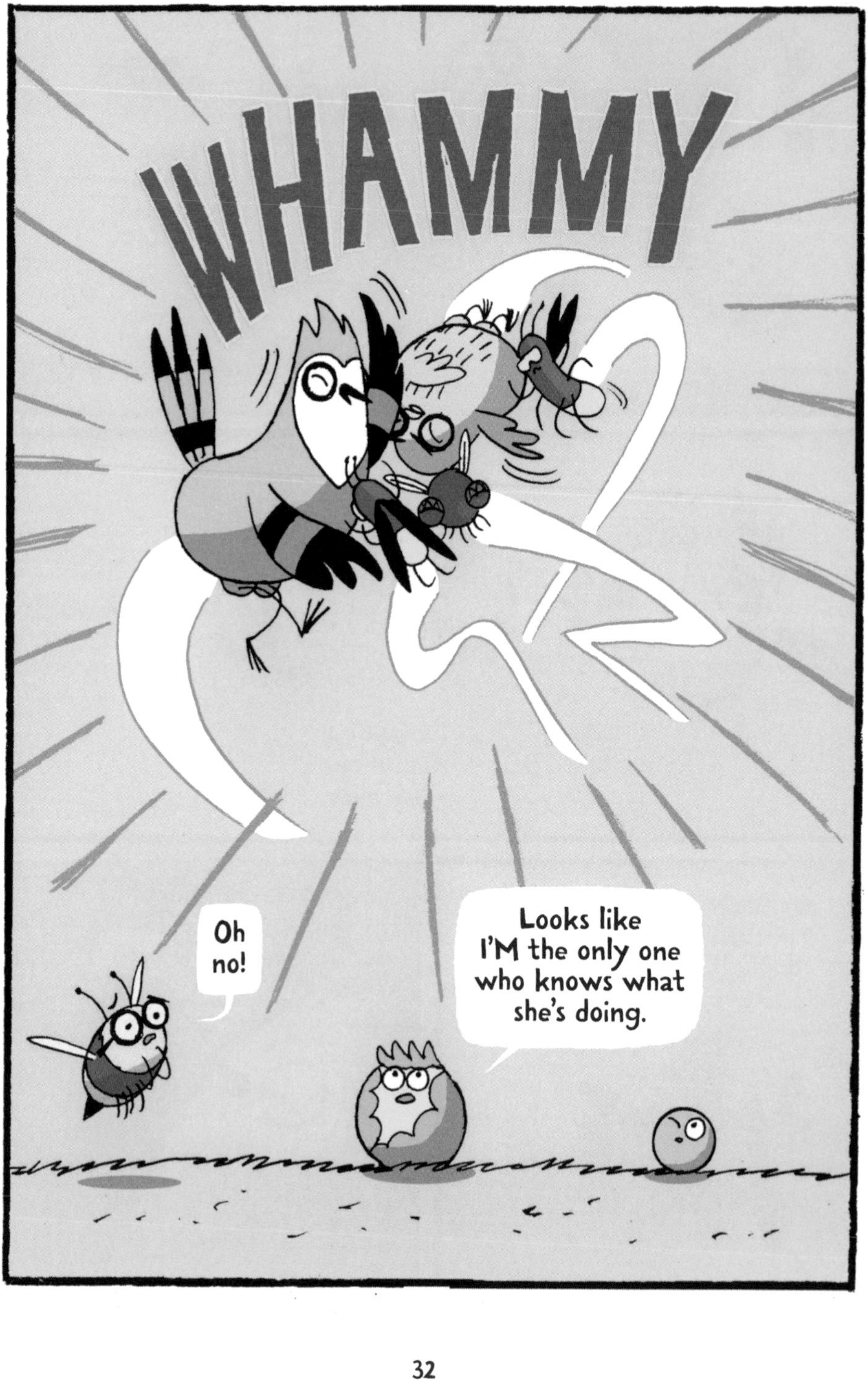
WHAMMY
Oh no!
Looks like I'M the only one who knows what she's doing.

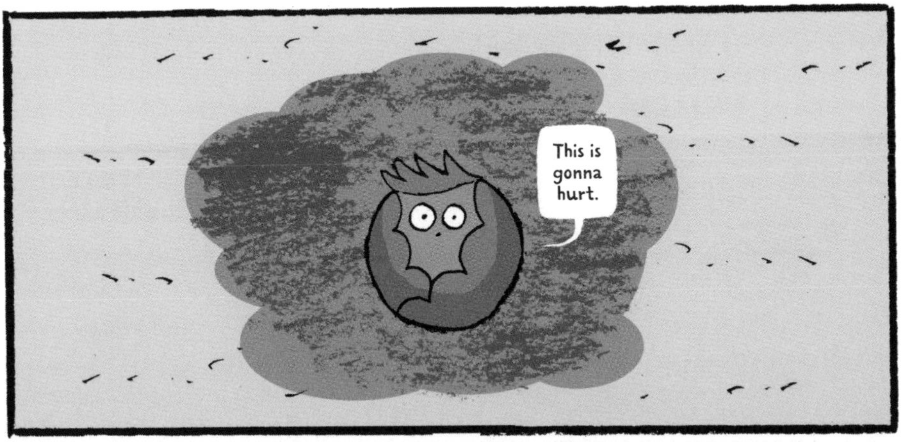
This is gonna hurt.

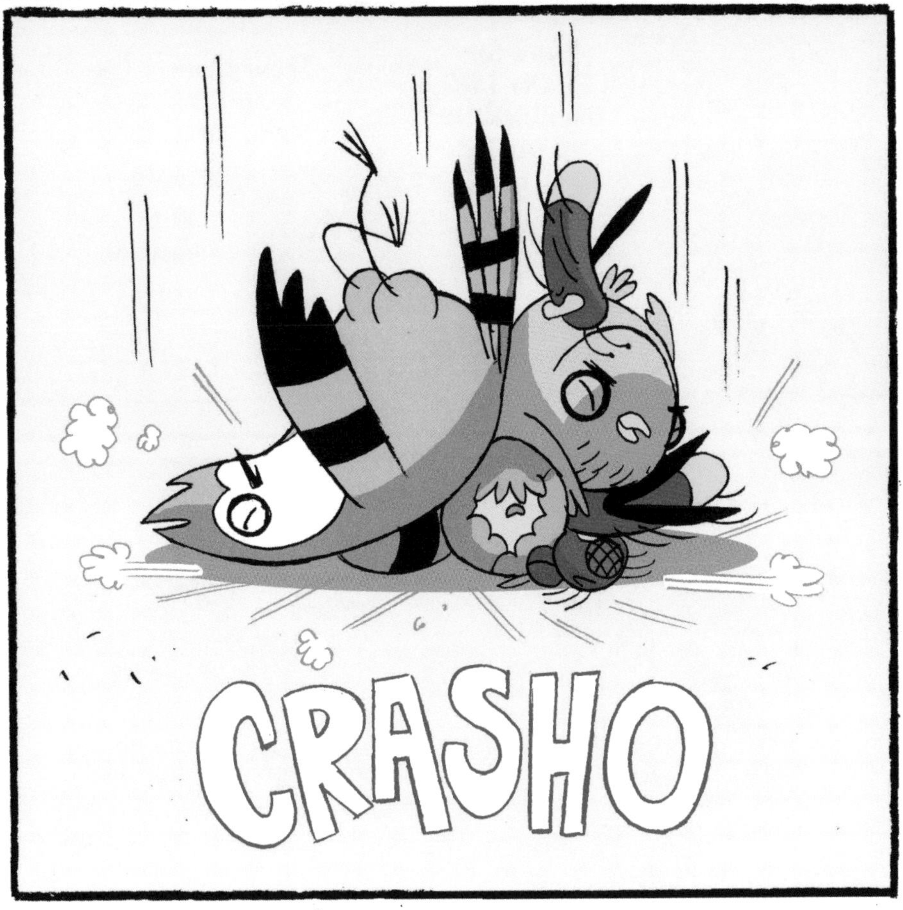
CRASHO

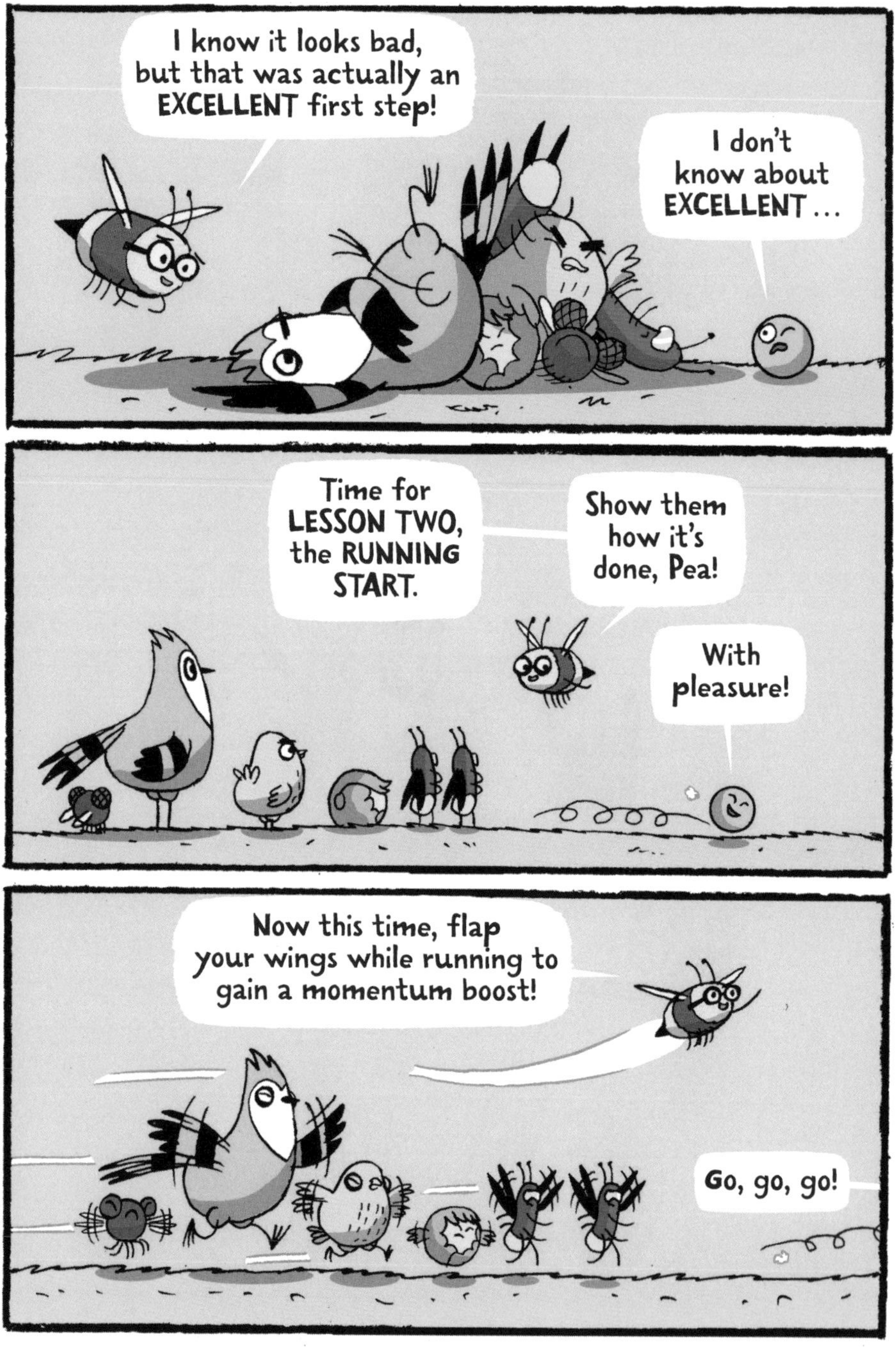
I know it looks bad, but that was actually an EXCELLENT first step!
I don't know about EXCELLENT . . .
Time for LESSON TWO, the RUNNING START.
Show them how it's done, Pea!
With pleasure!
Now this time, flap your wings while running to gain a momentum boost!
Go, go, go!

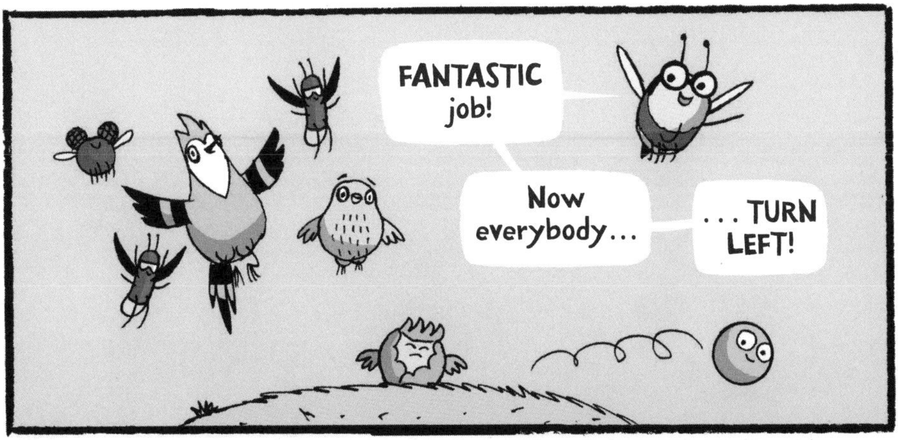
FANTASTIC job!
Now everybody...
...TURN LEFT!

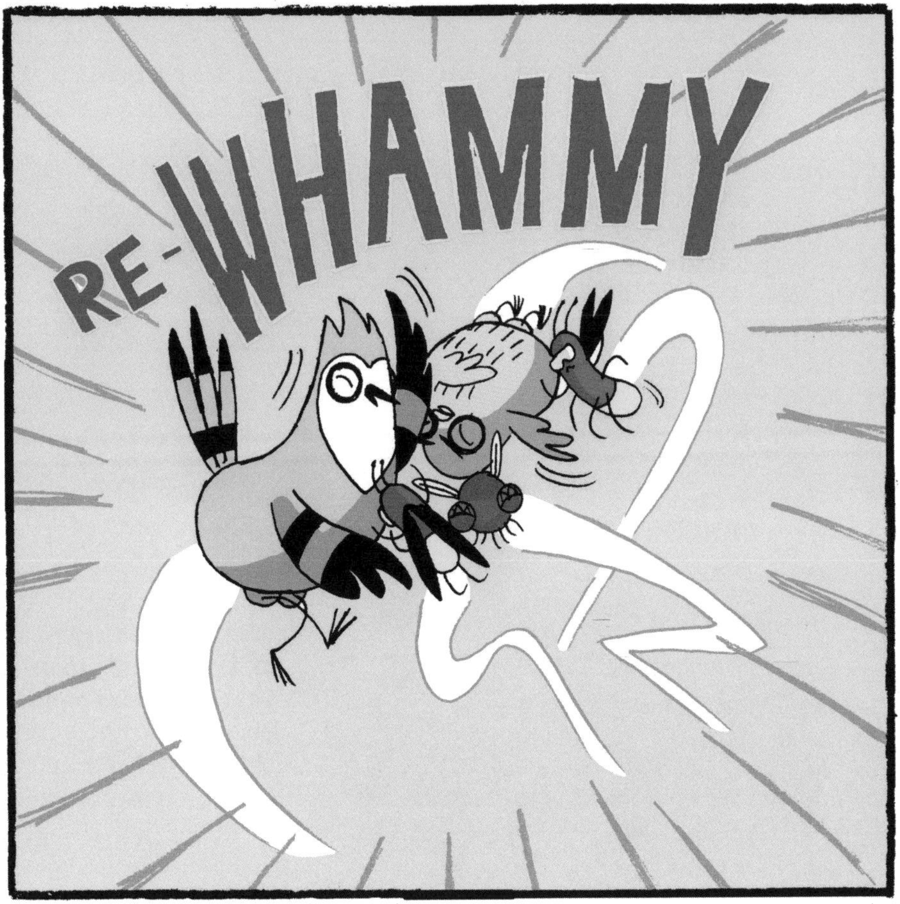
RE-WHAMMY

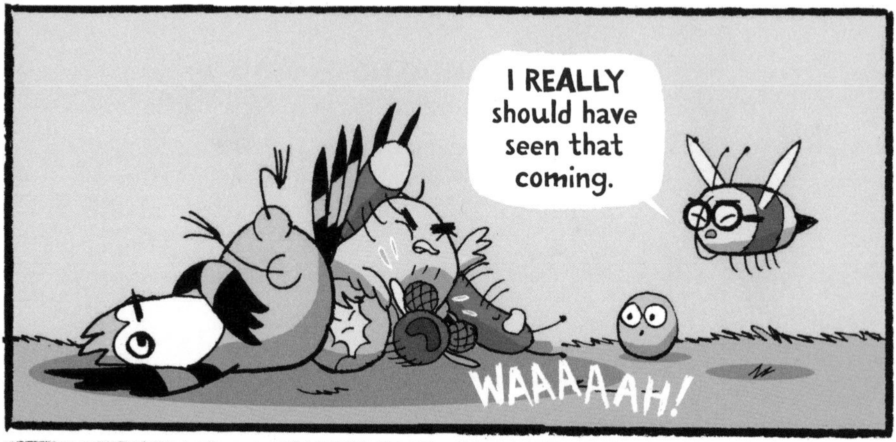
I REALLY should have seen that coming.
WAAAAAH!

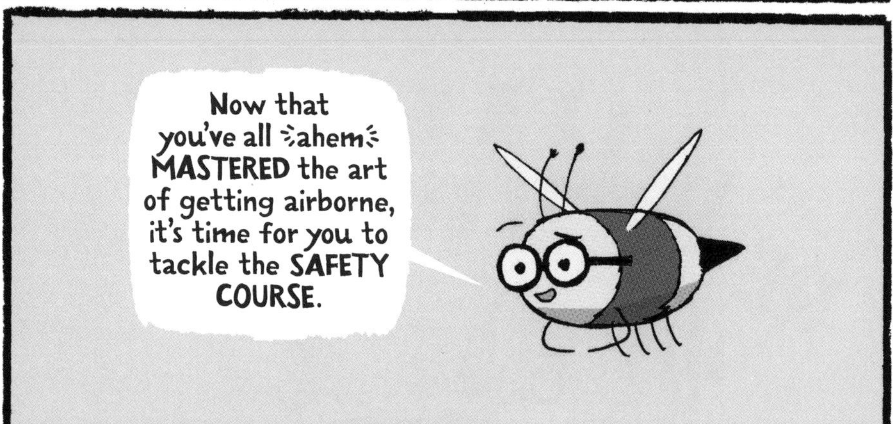
Now that you've all ahem MASTERED the art of getting airborne, it's time for you to tackle the SAFETY COURSE.

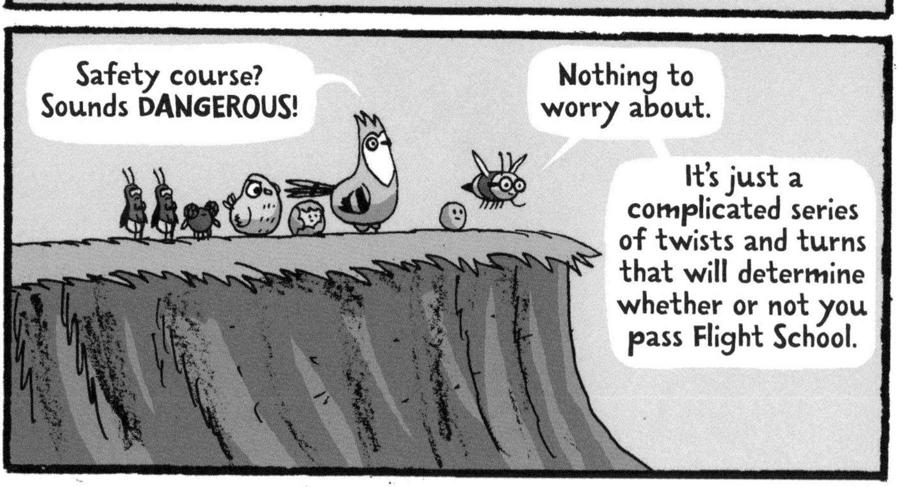
Safety course? Sounds DANGEROUS!
Nothing to worry about.
It's just a complicated series of twists and turns that will determine whether or not you pass Flight School.

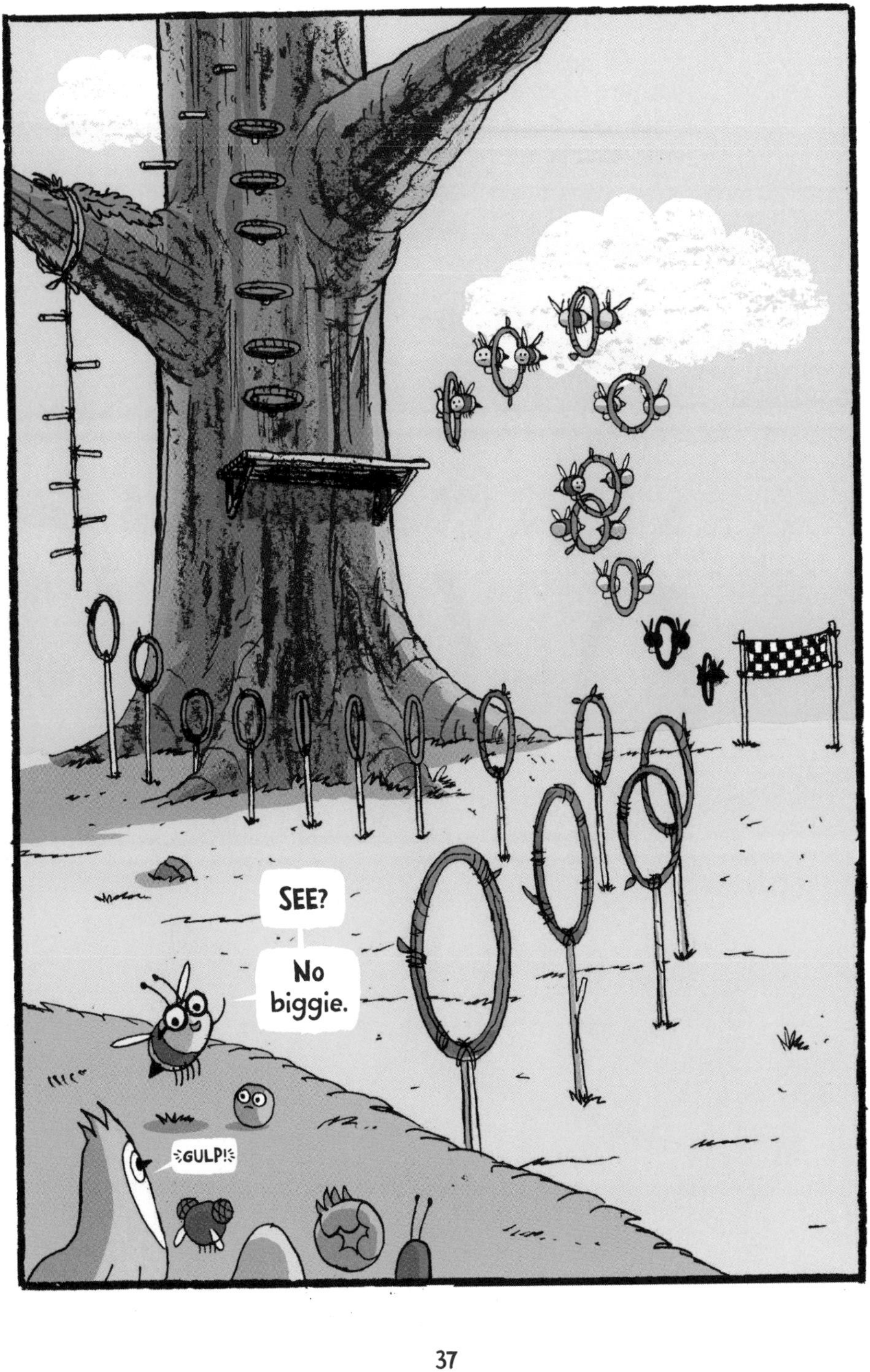
SEE?
No biggie.
GULP!

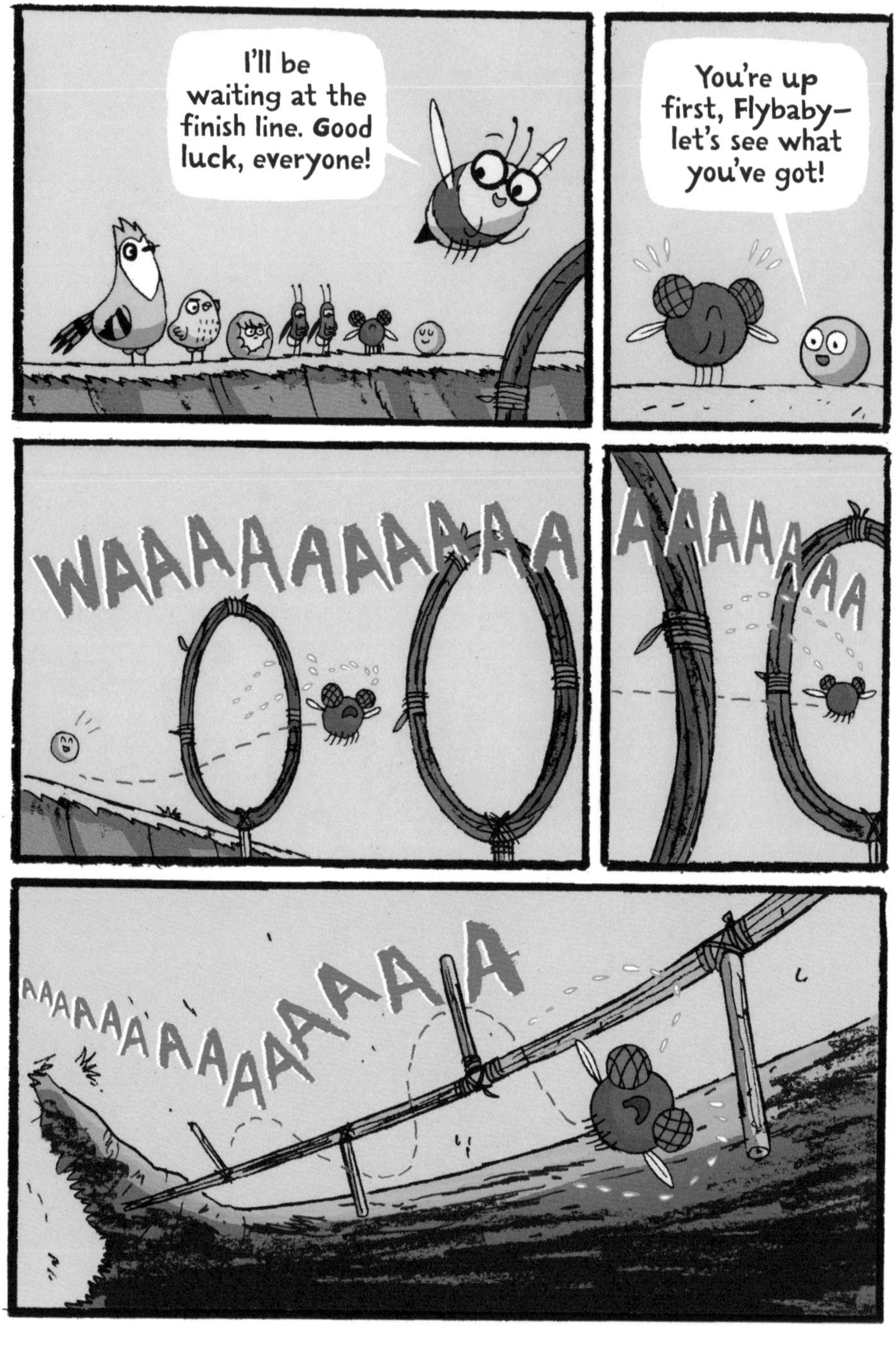
I'll be waiting at the finish line. Good luck, everyone!
You're up first, Flybaby—let's see what you've got!
WAAAAAAAAAA
AAAAAAAA
AAAAAAAAAAAAAA

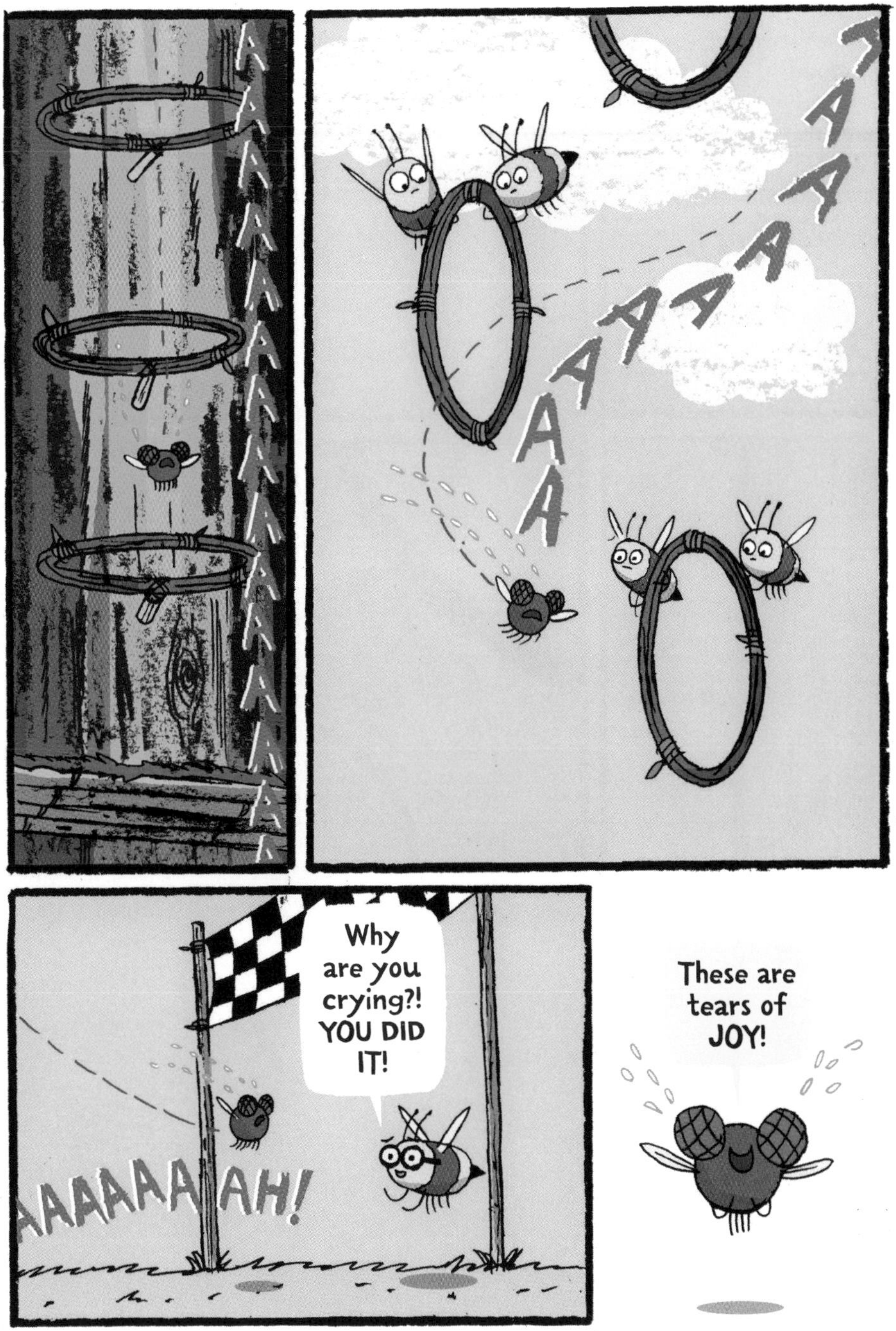
Why are you crying?! YOU DID IT!
AAAAAAAH!
These are tears of JOY!

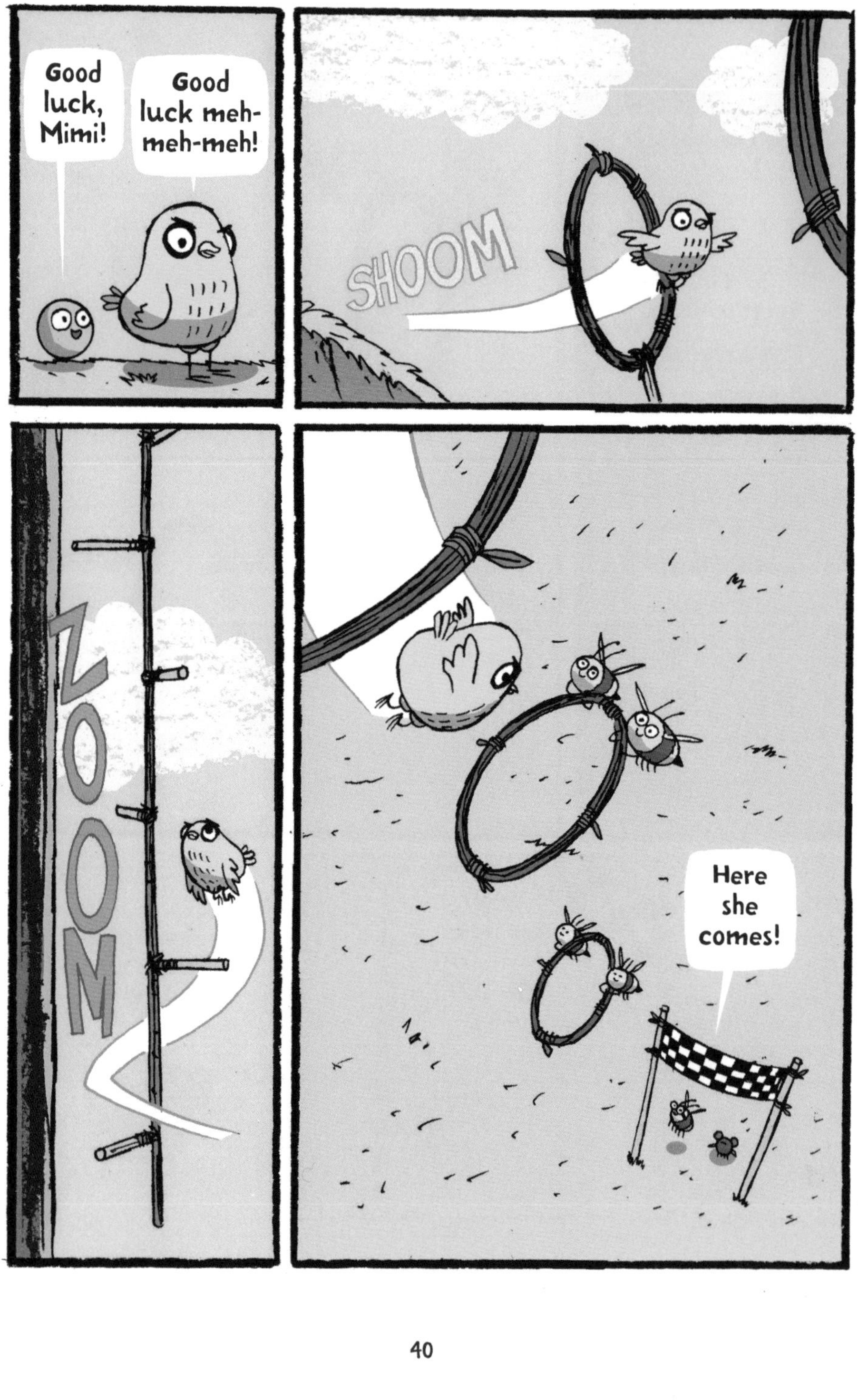
Good luck, Mimi!
Good luck meh-meh-meh!
SHOOM
ZOOM
Here she comes!

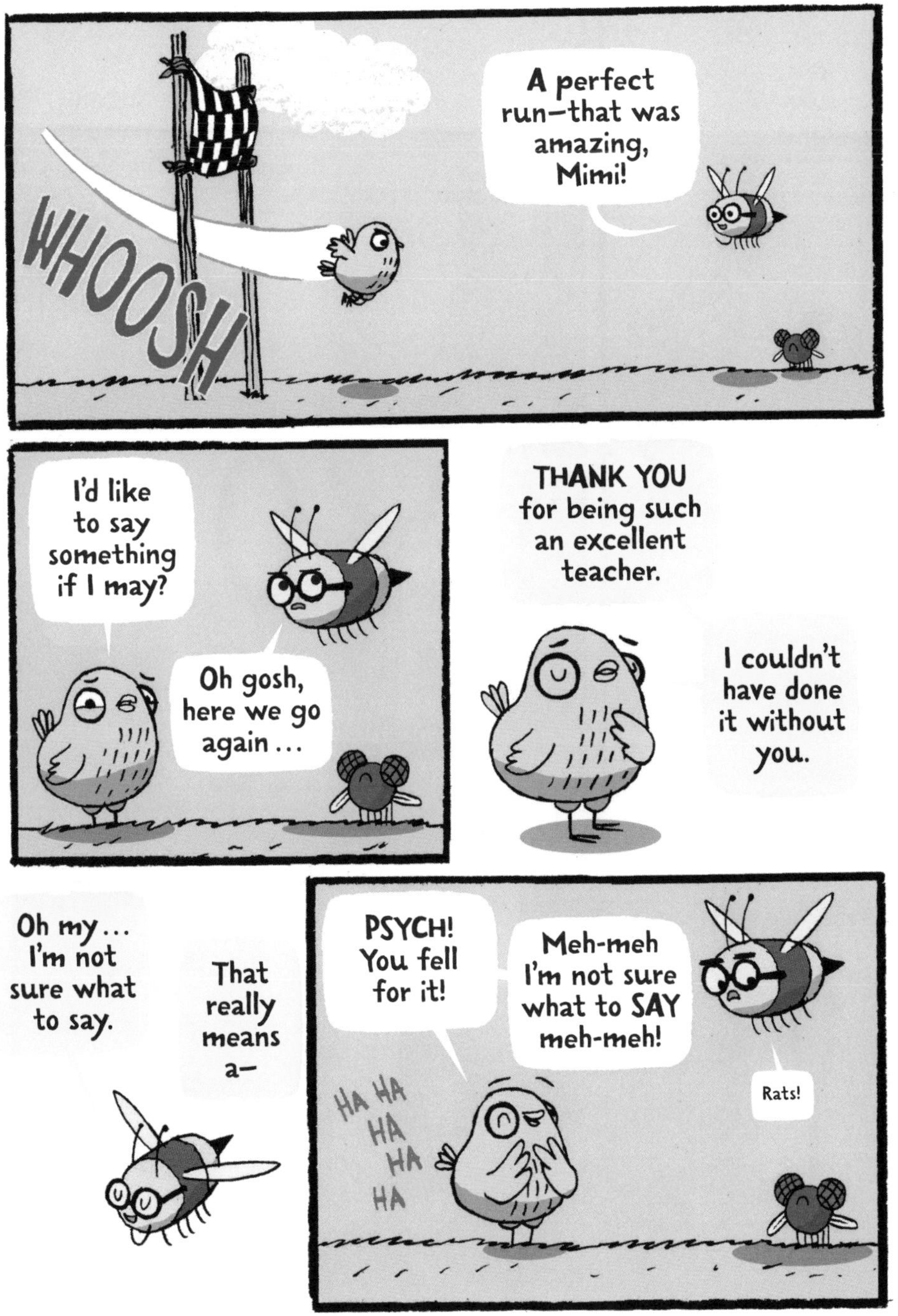

WHOOSH
A perfect run—that was amazing, Mimi!
I'd like to say something if I may?
Oh gosh, here we go again . . .
THANK YOU for being such an excellent teacher.
I couldn't have done it without you.
Oh my . . . I'm not sure what to say.
That really means a—
PSYCH! You fell for it!
HA HA HA HA HA
Meh-meh I'm not sure what to SAY meh-meh!
Rats!

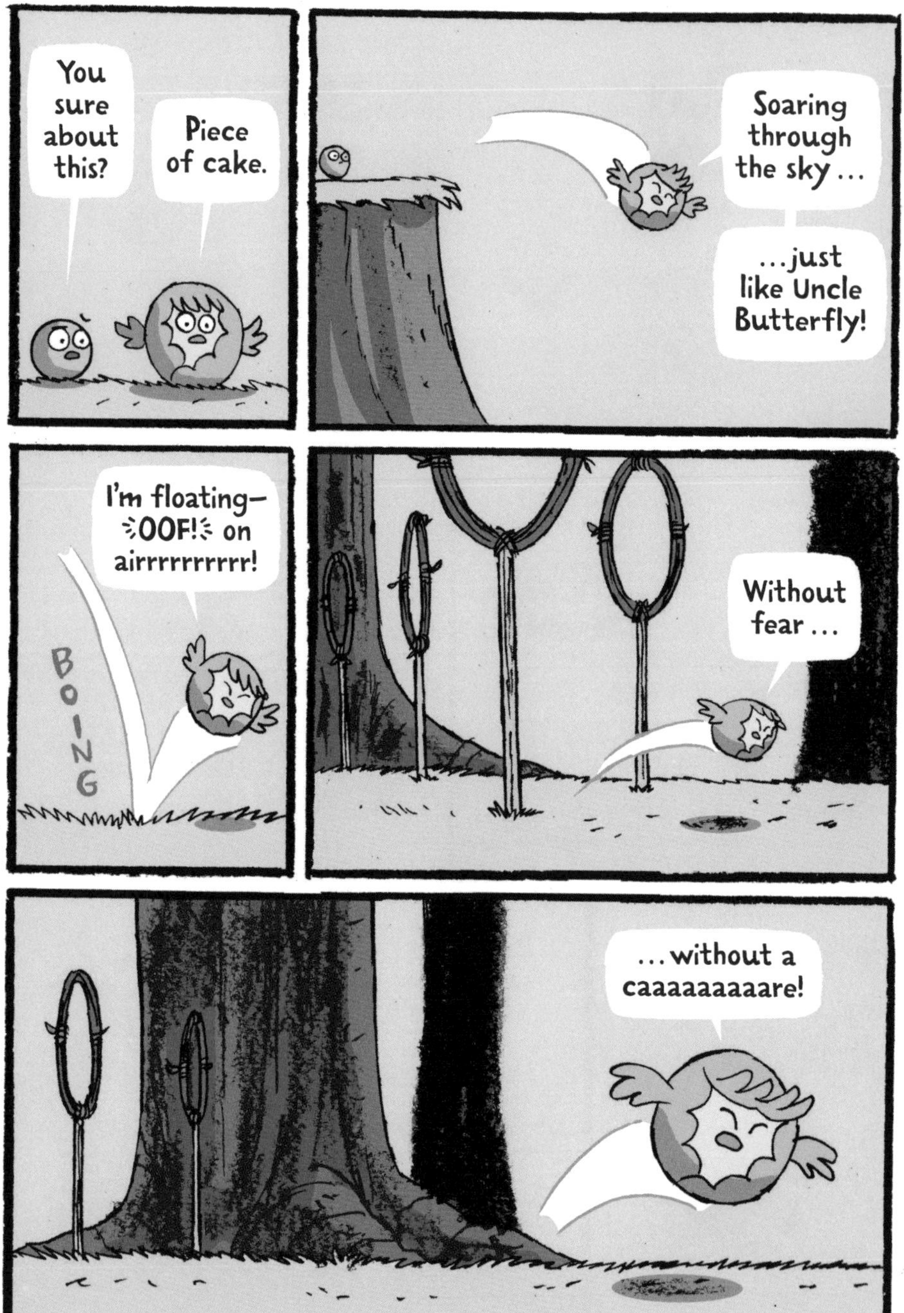
You sure about this?
Piece of cake.
Soaring through the sky . . .
. . . just like Uncle Butterfly!
I'm floating— OOF! on airrrrrrrrrr!
BOING
Without fear . . .
. . . without a caaaaaaaaare!

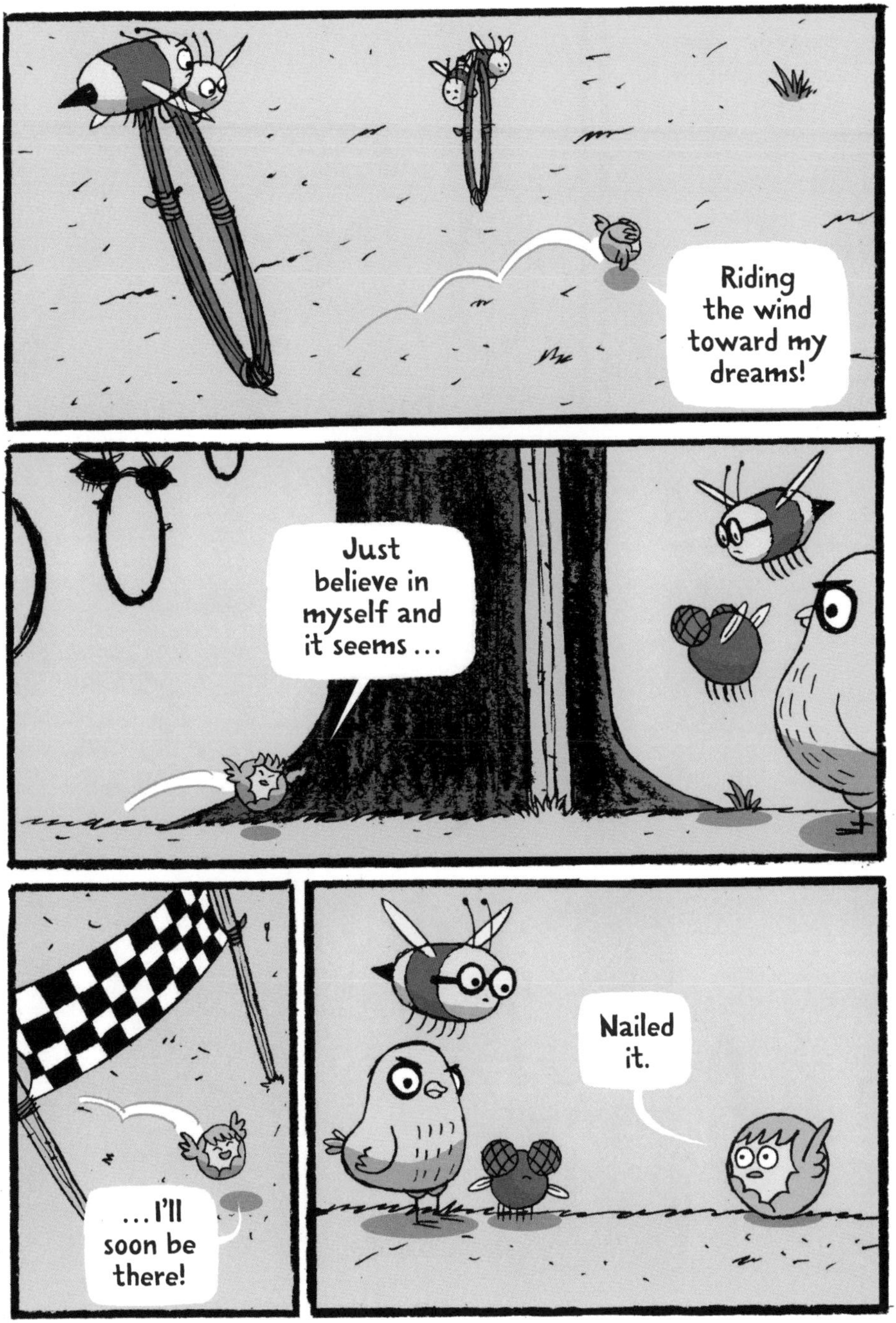
Riding the wind toward my dreams!
Just believe in myself and it seems…
…I'll soon be there!
Nailed it.

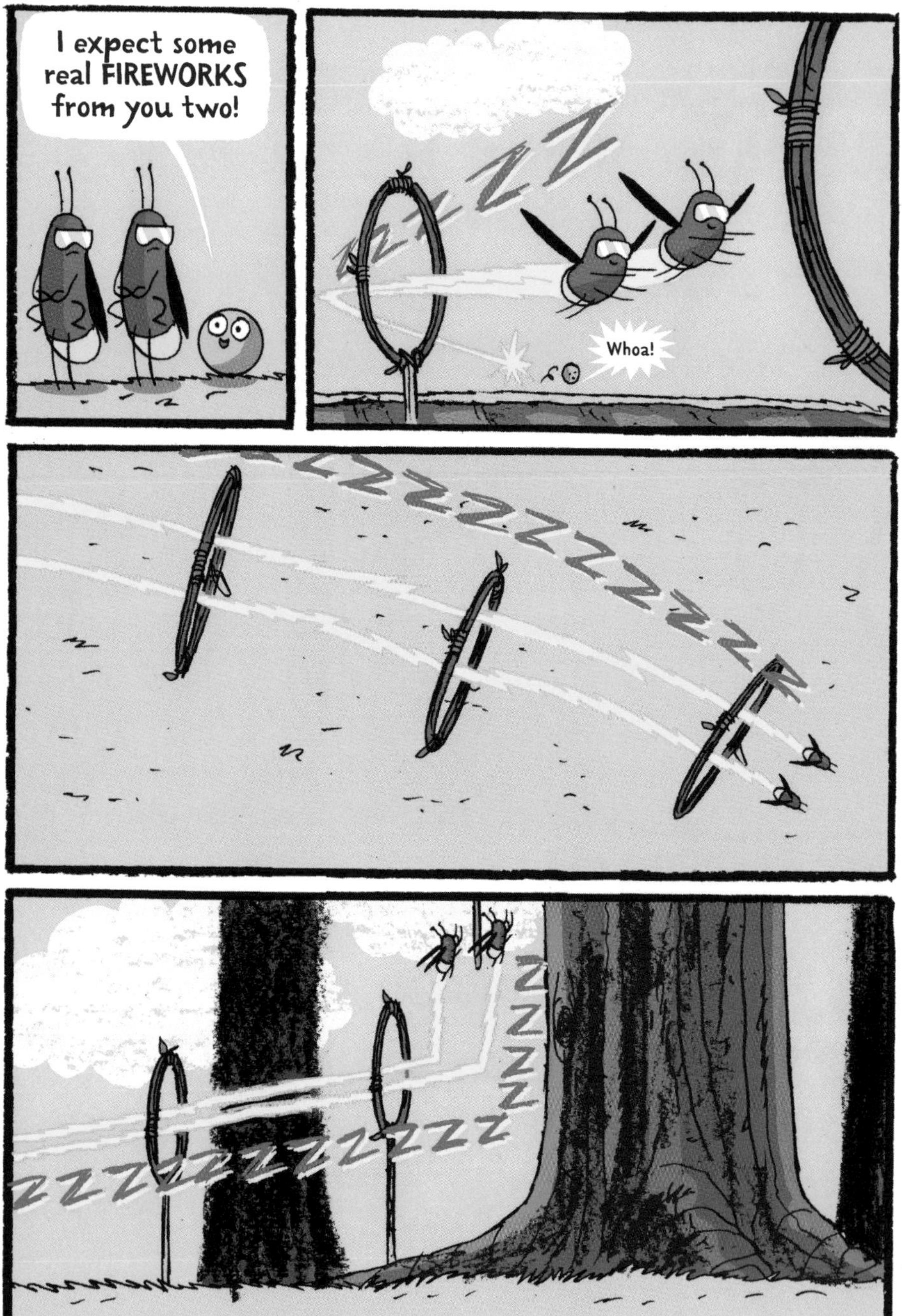
I expect some real FIREWORKS from you two!
Whoa!

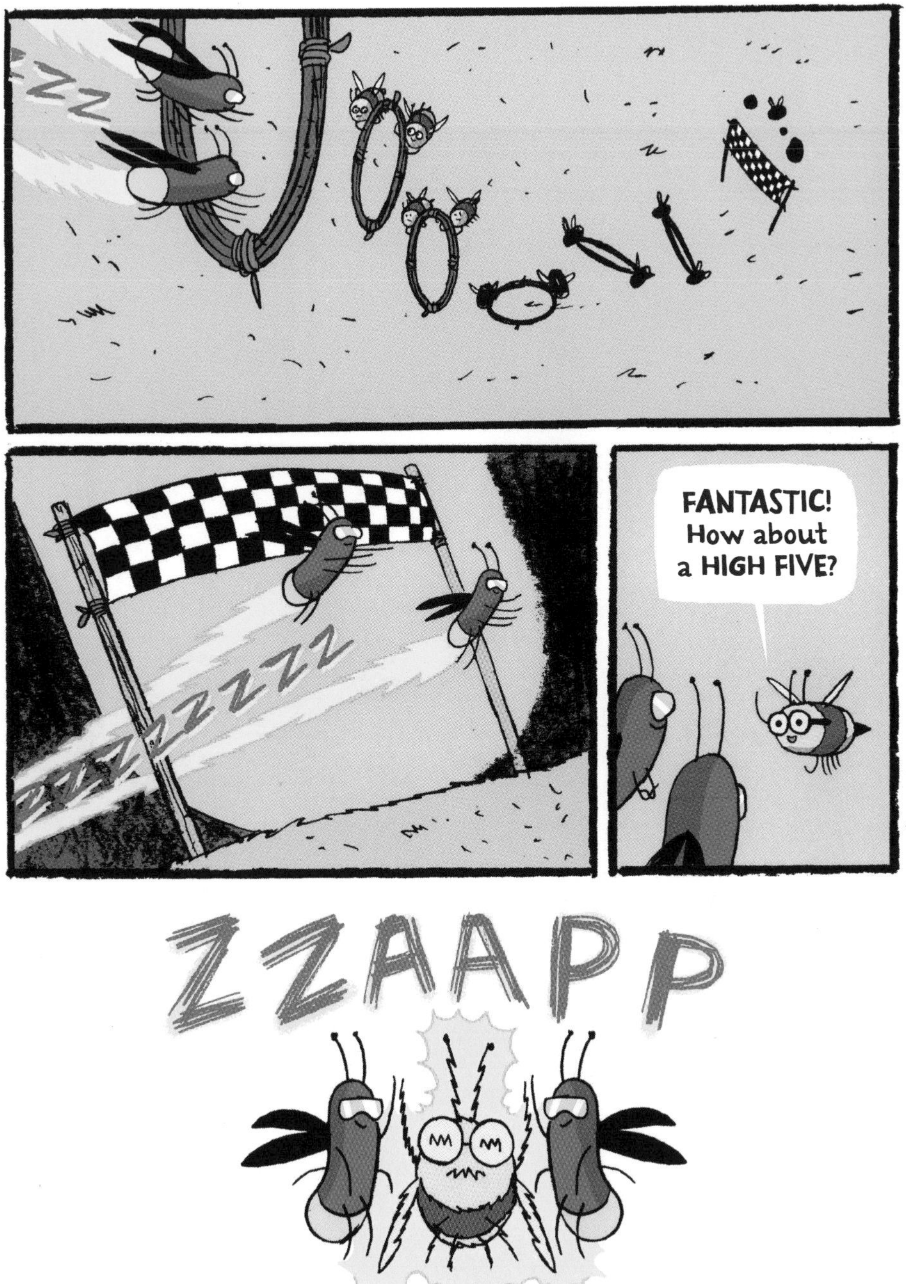

ZZZ
ZZZZZZZZZZZ
FANTASTIC! How about a HIGH FIVE?
ZZAAPP

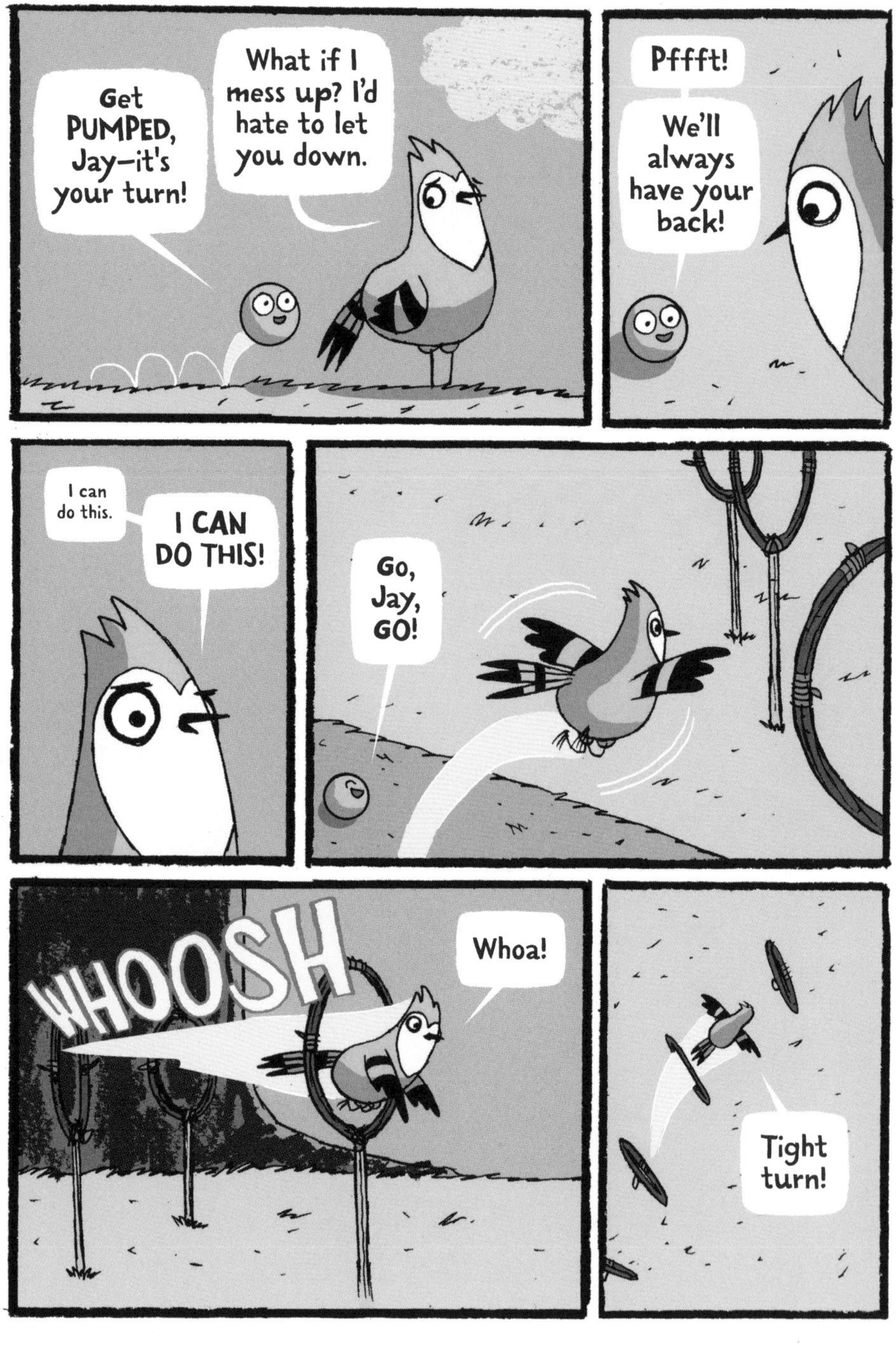
Get PUMPED, Jay—it's your turn!
What if I mess up? I'd hate to let you down.
Pffft!
We'll always have your back!
I can do this.
I CAN DO THIS!
Go, Jay, GO!
WHOOSH
Whoa!
Tight turn!

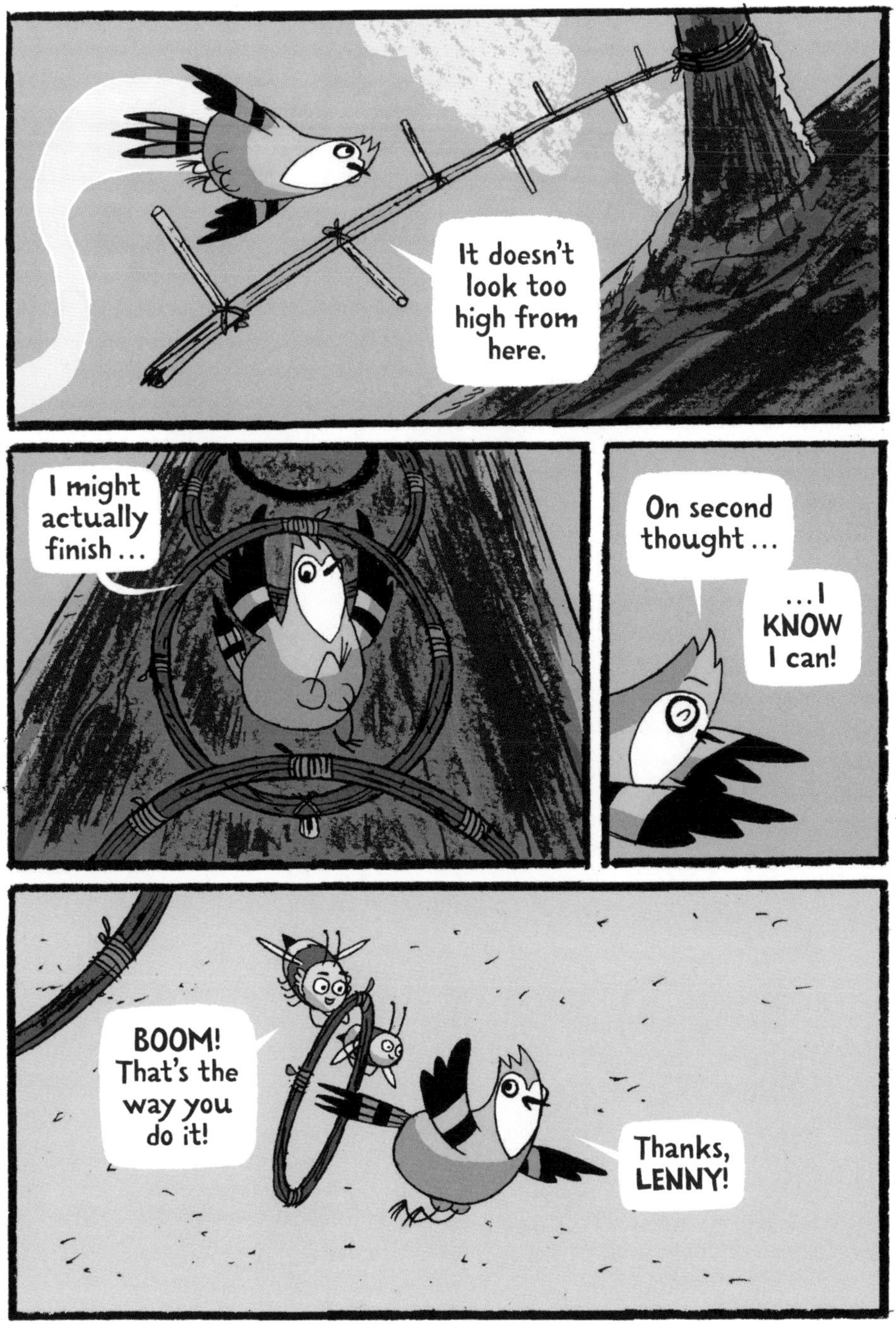
It doesn't look too high from here.
I might actually finish ...
On second thought ...
... I KNOW I can!
BOOM! That's the way you do it!
Thanks, LENNY!

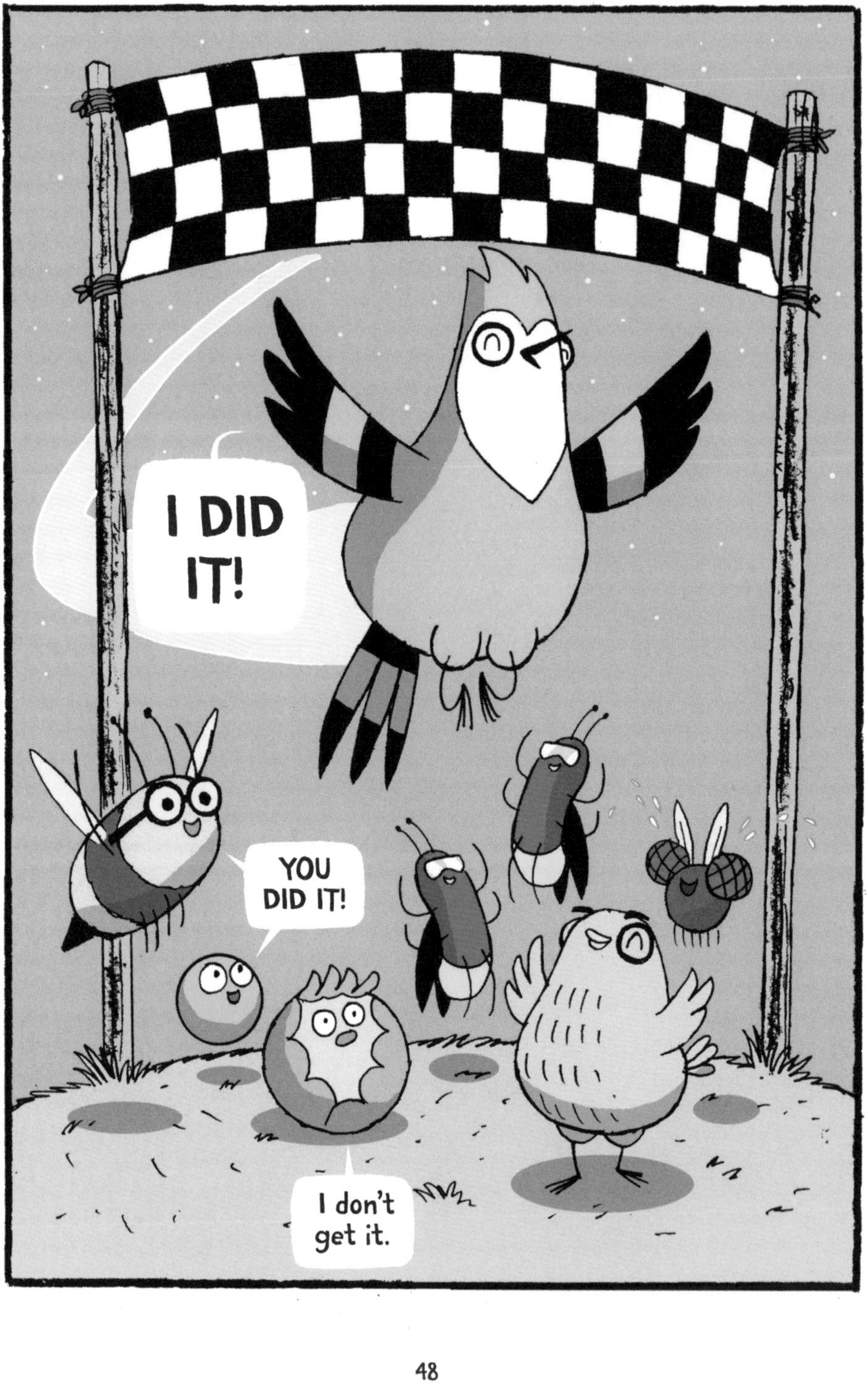
I DID IT!
YOU DID IT!
I don't get it.

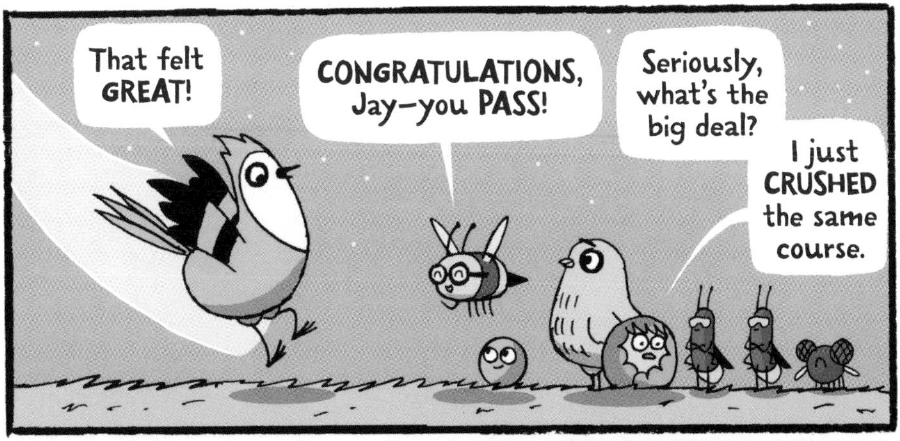
That felt GREAT!
CONGRATULATIONS, Jay—you PASS!
Seriously, what's the big deal?
I just CRUSHED the same course.

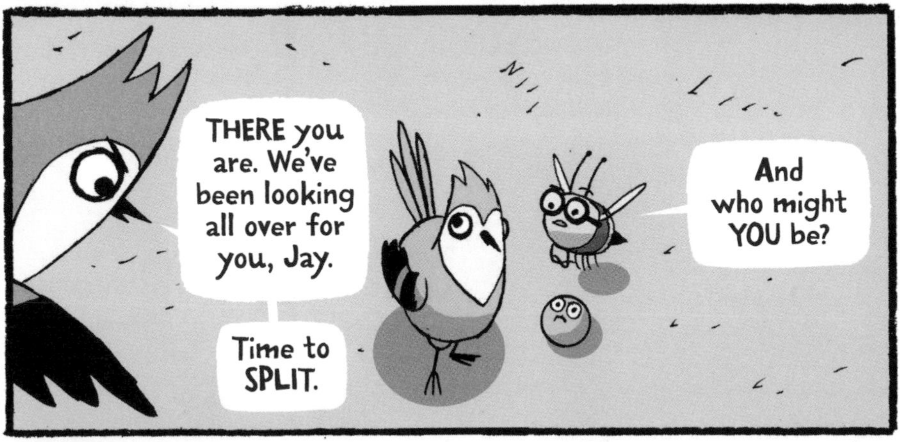
THERE you are. We've been looking all over for you, Jay.
Time to SPLIT.
And who might YOU be?

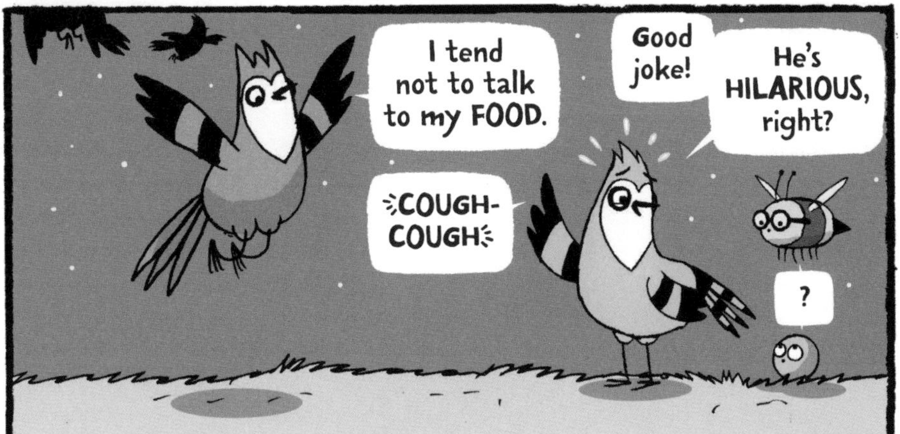
I tend not to talk to my FOOD.
Good joke!
He's HILARIOUS, right?
COUGH-COUGH
?

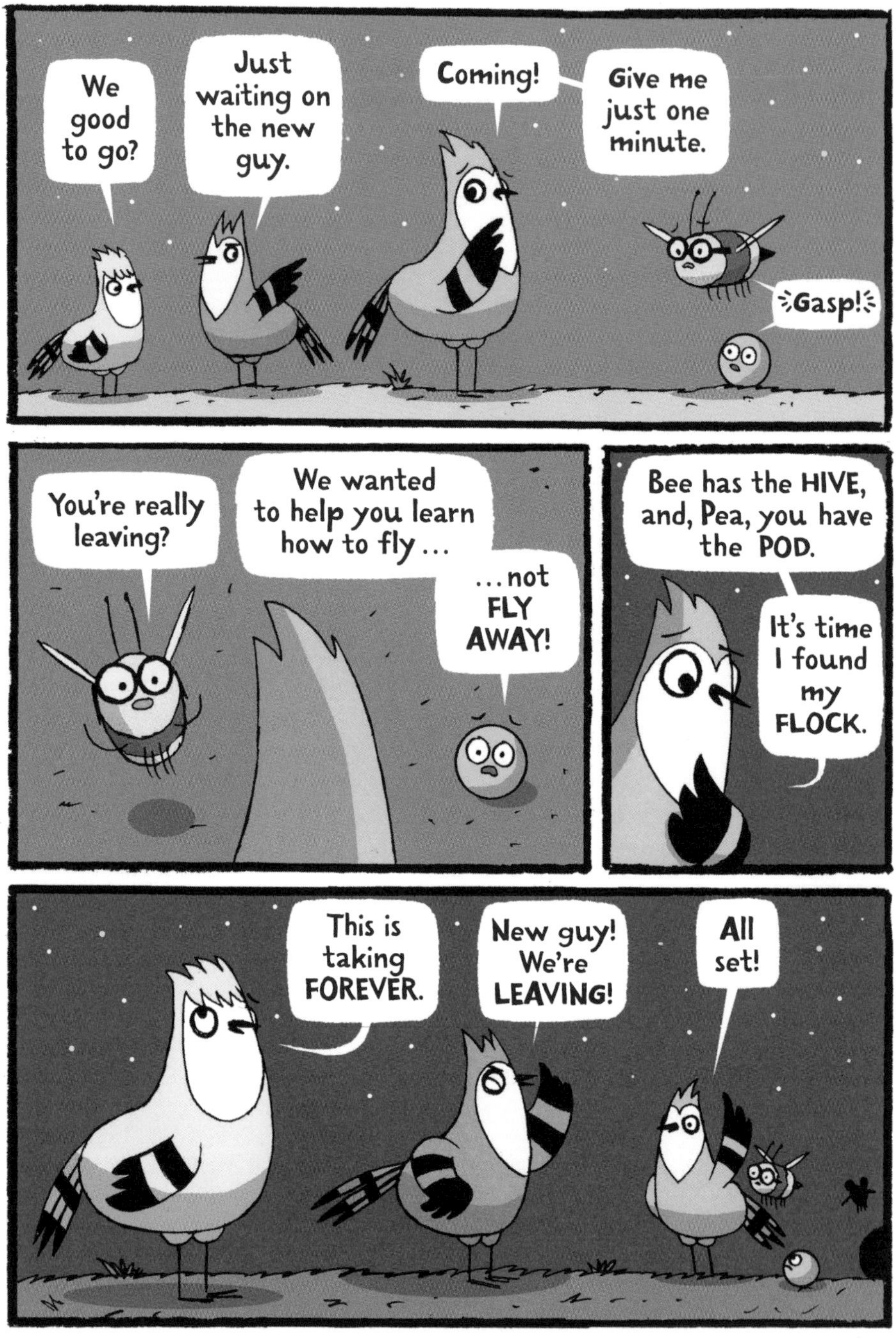
We good to go?
Just waiting on the new guy.
Coming!
Give me just one minute.
Gasp!
You're really leaving?
We wanted to help you learn how to fly...
...not FLY AWAY!
Bee has the HIVE, and, Pea, you have the POD.
It's time I found my FLOCK.
This is taking FOREVER.
New guy! We're LEAVING!
All set!

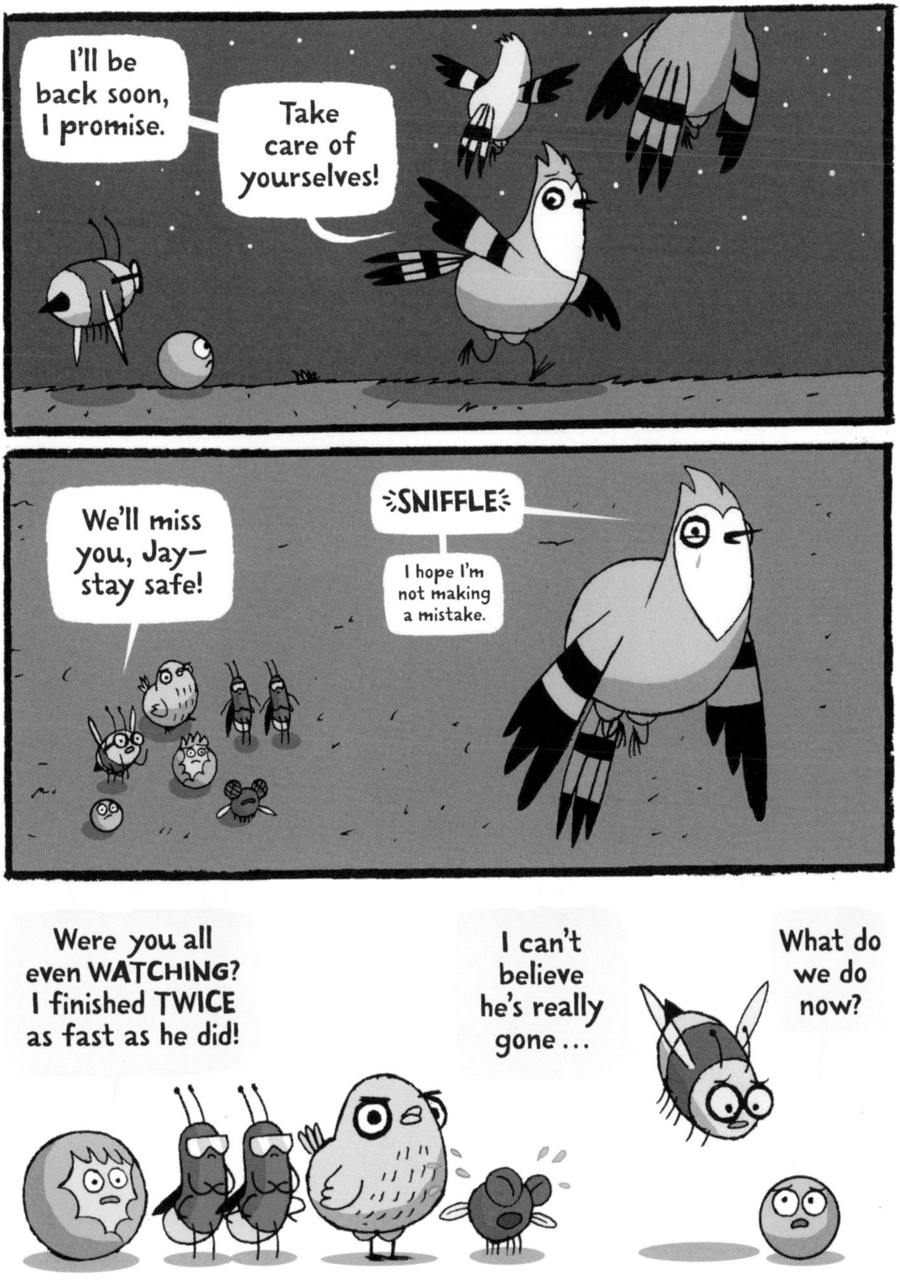
I'll be back soon, I promise.
Take care of yourselves!
We'll miss you, Jay— stay safe!
SNIFFLE
I hope I'm not making a mistake.
Were you all even WATCHING? I finished TWICE as fast as he did!
I can't believe he's really gone . . .
What do we do now?

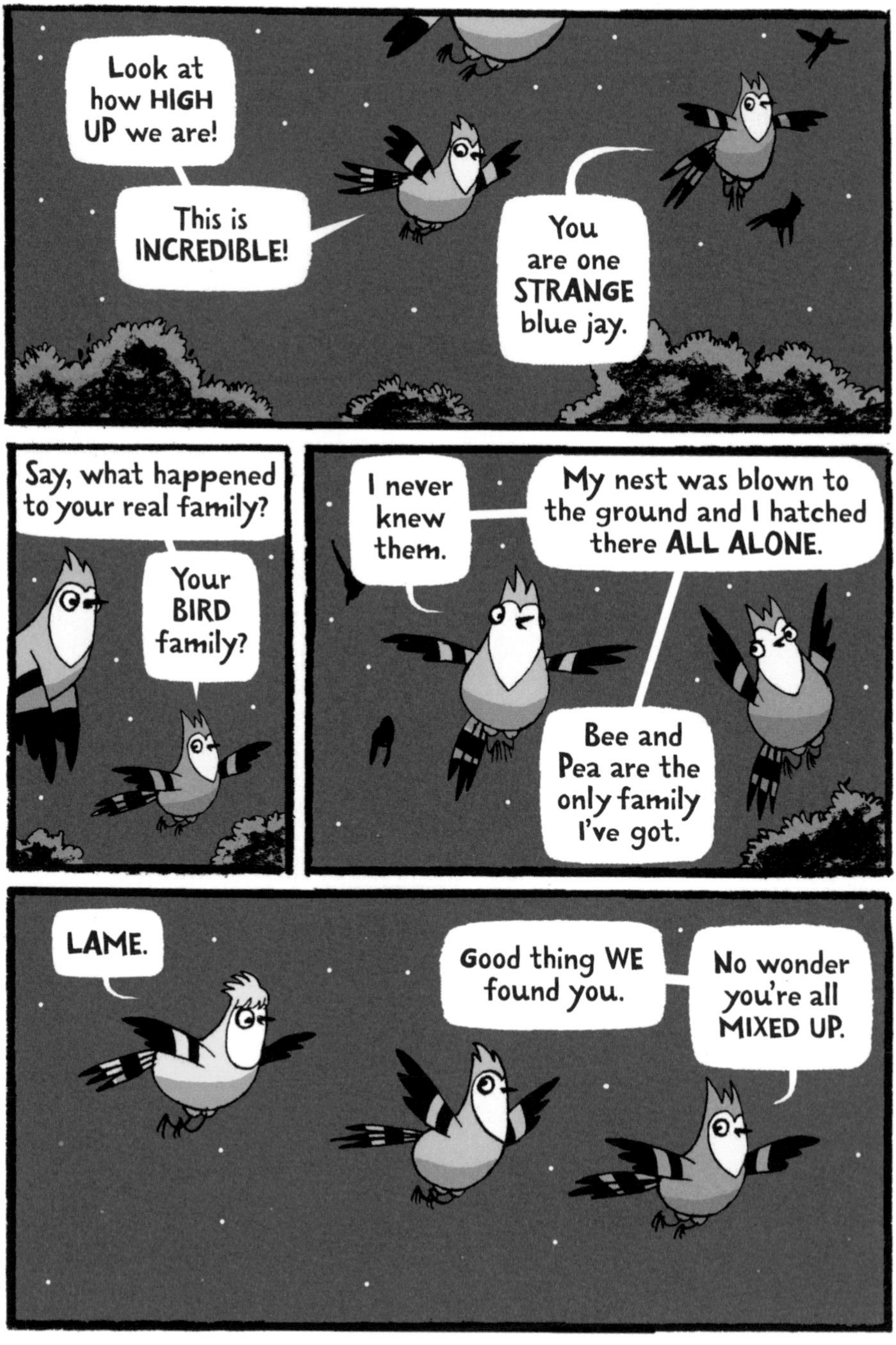
Look at how HIGH UP we are!
This is INCREDIBLE!
You are one STRANGE blue jay.
Say, what happened to your real family?
Your BIRD family?
I never knew them.
My nest was blown to the ground and I hatched there ALL ALONE.
Bee and Pea are the only family I've got.
LAME.
Good thing WE found you.
No wonder you're all MIXED UP.

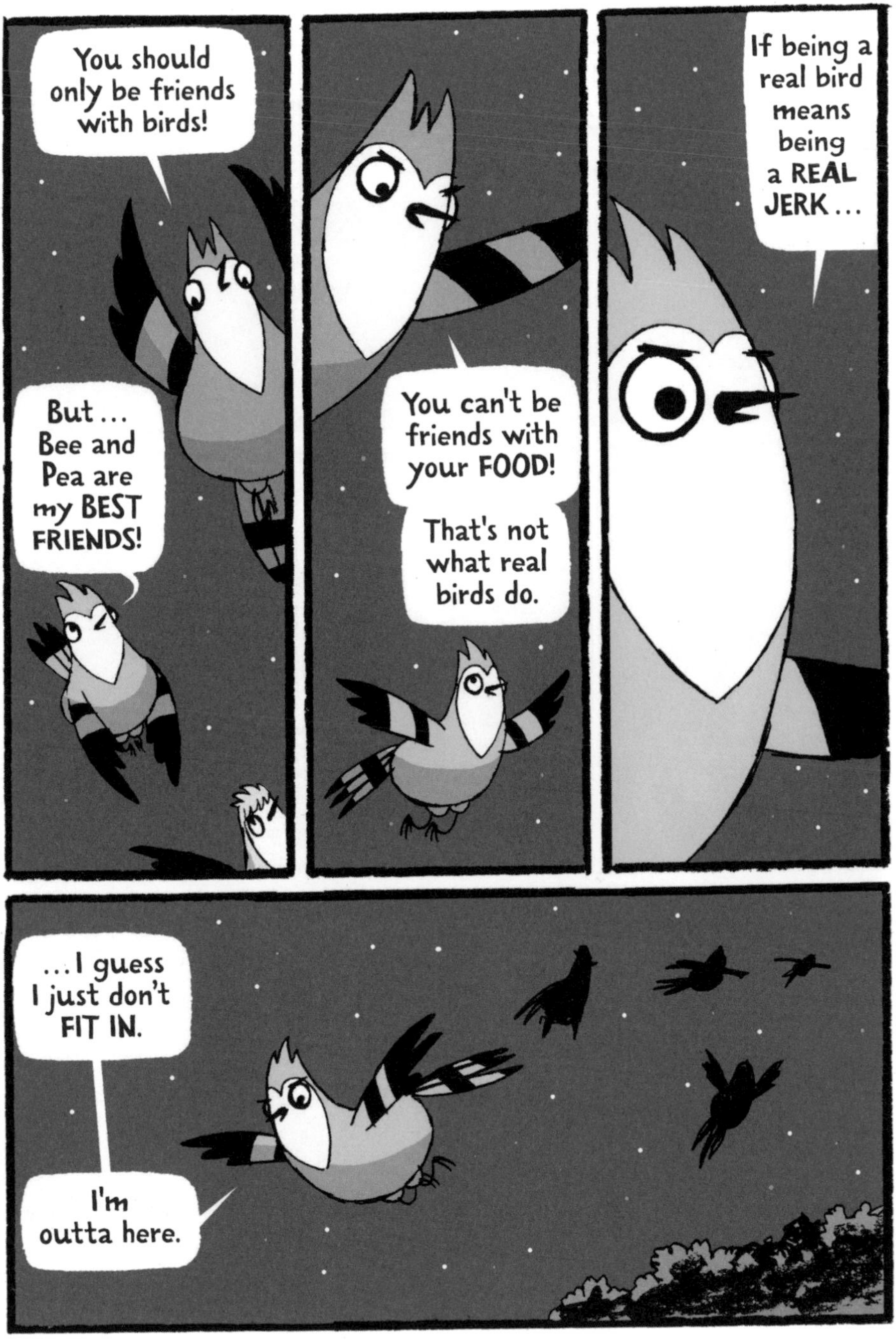
You should only be friends with birds!
But... Bee and Pea are my BEST FRIENDS!
You can't be friends with your FOOD!
That's not what real birds do.
If being a real bird means being a REAL JERK...
...I guess I just don't FIT IN.
I'm outta here.

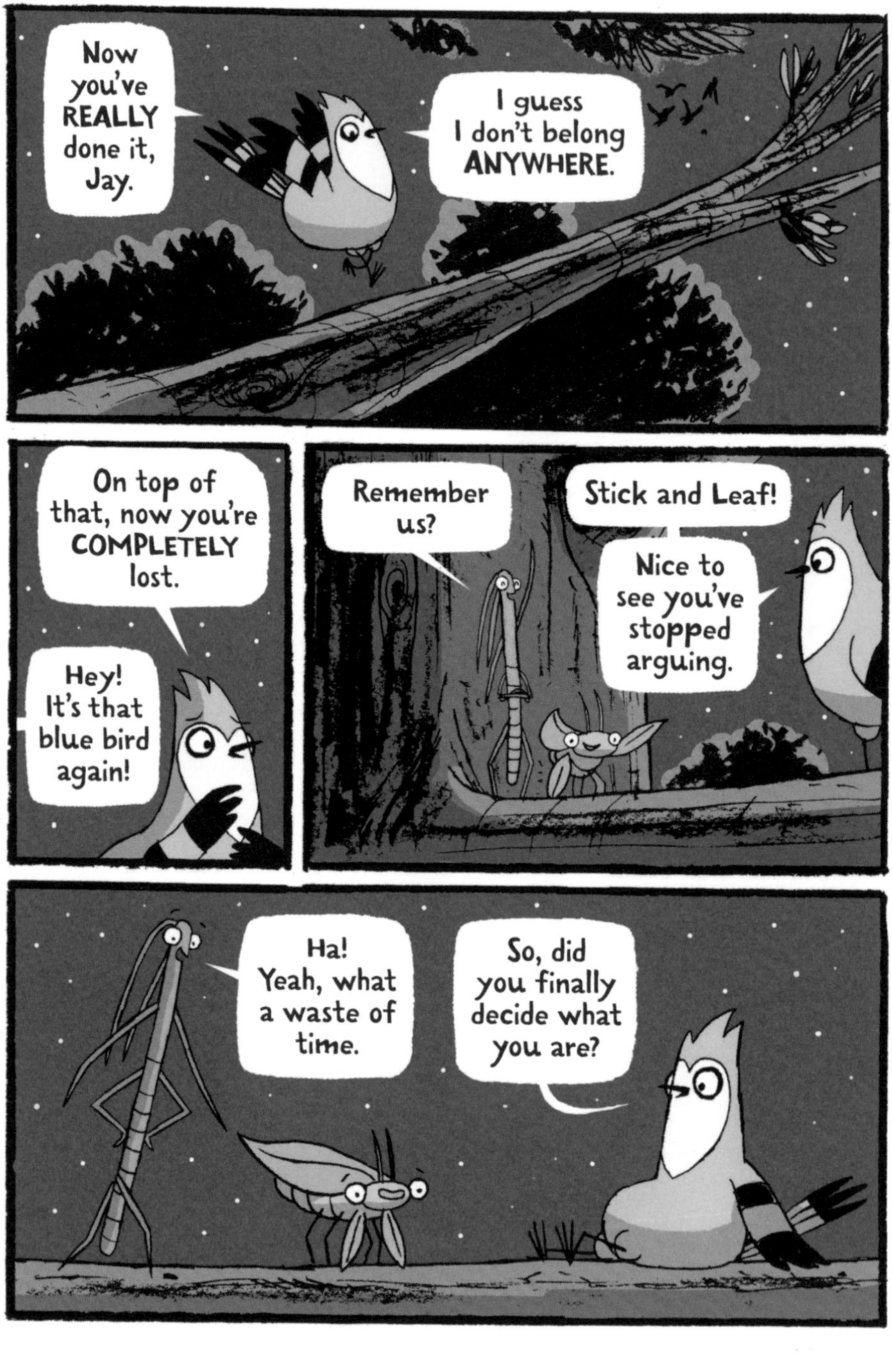
Now you've REALLY done it, Jay.
I guess I don't belong ANYWHERE.
On top of that, now you're COMPLETELY lost.
Hey! It's that blue bird again!
Remember us?
Stick and Leaf!
Nice to see you've stopped arguing.
Ha! Yeah, what a waste of time.
So, did you finally decide what you are?

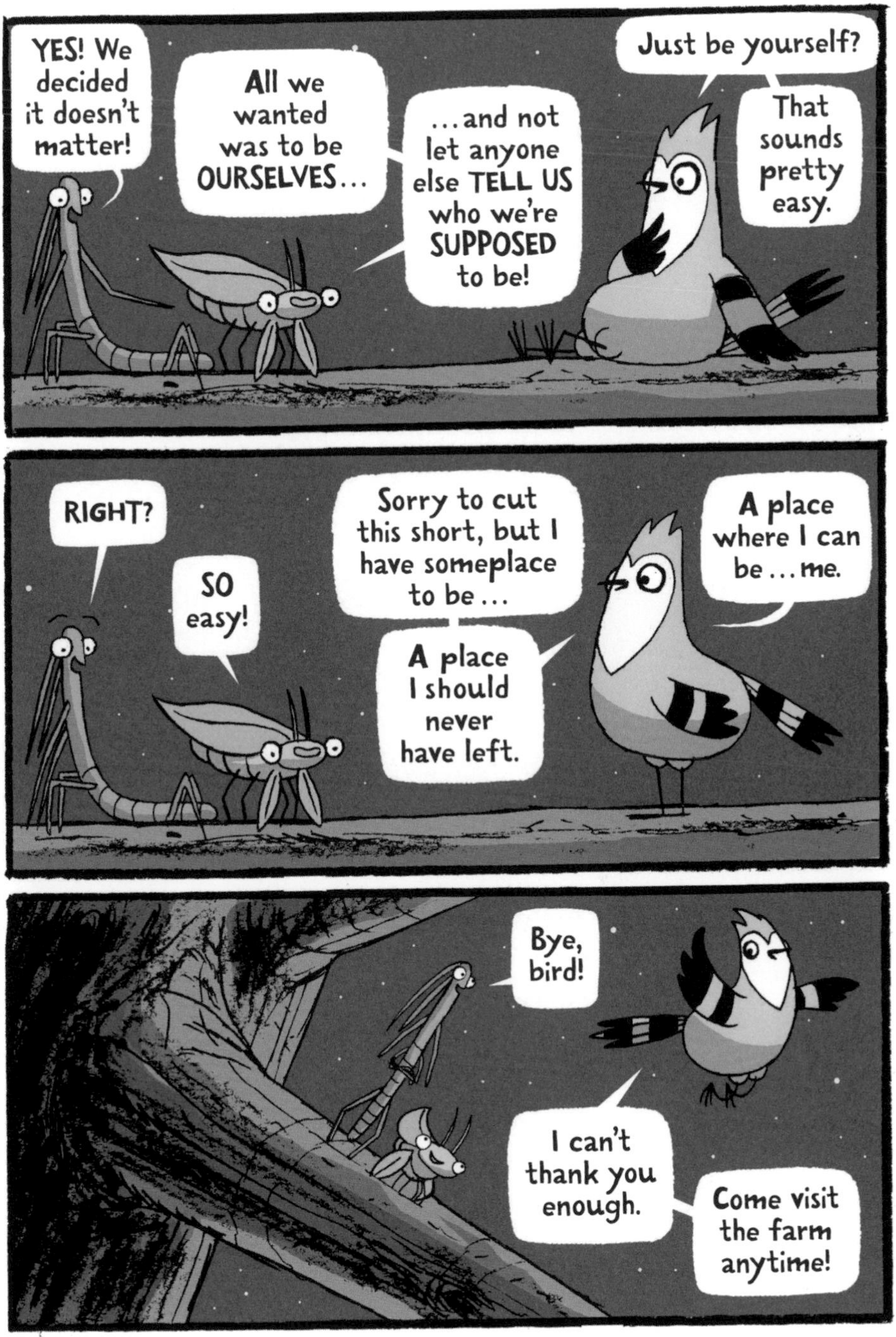
YES! We decided it doesn't matter!
All we wanted was to be OURSELVES...
...and not let anyone else TELL US who we're SUPPOSED to be!
Just be yourself?
That sounds pretty easy.
RIGHT?
SO easy!
Sorry to cut this short, but I have someplace to be...
A place I should never have left.
A place where I can be...me.
Bye, bird!
I can't thank you enough.
Come visit the farm anytime!

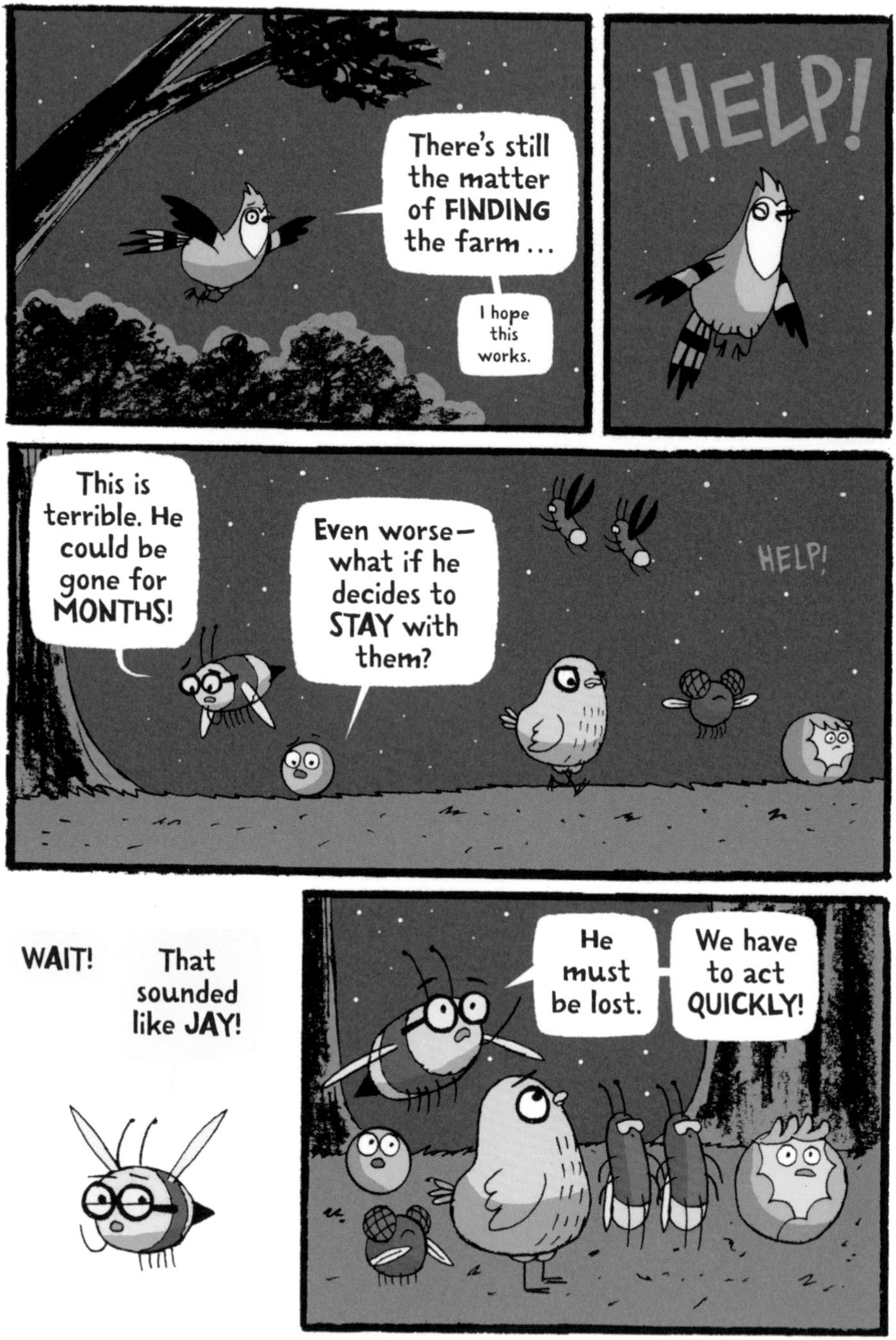
There's still the matter of FINDING the farm . . .
I hope this works.
HELP!
This is terrible. He could be gone for MONTHS!
Even worse— what if he decides to STAY with them?
HELP!
WAIT! That sounded like JAY!
He must be lost.
We have to act QUICKLY!

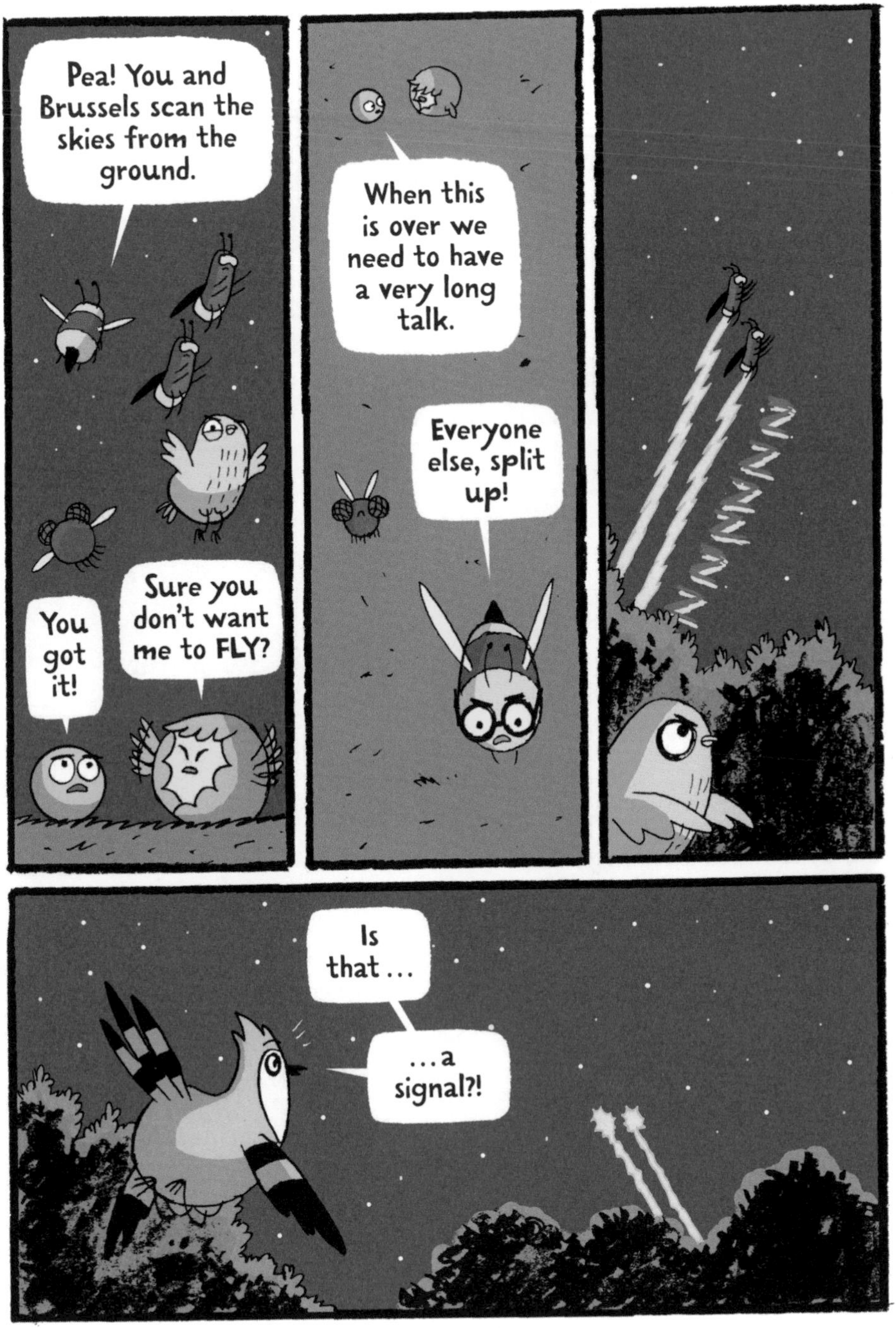
Pea! You and Brussels scan the skies from the ground.
You got it!
Sure you don't want me to FLY?
When this is over we need to have a very long talk.
Everyone else, split up!
Is that . . .
. . . a signal?!

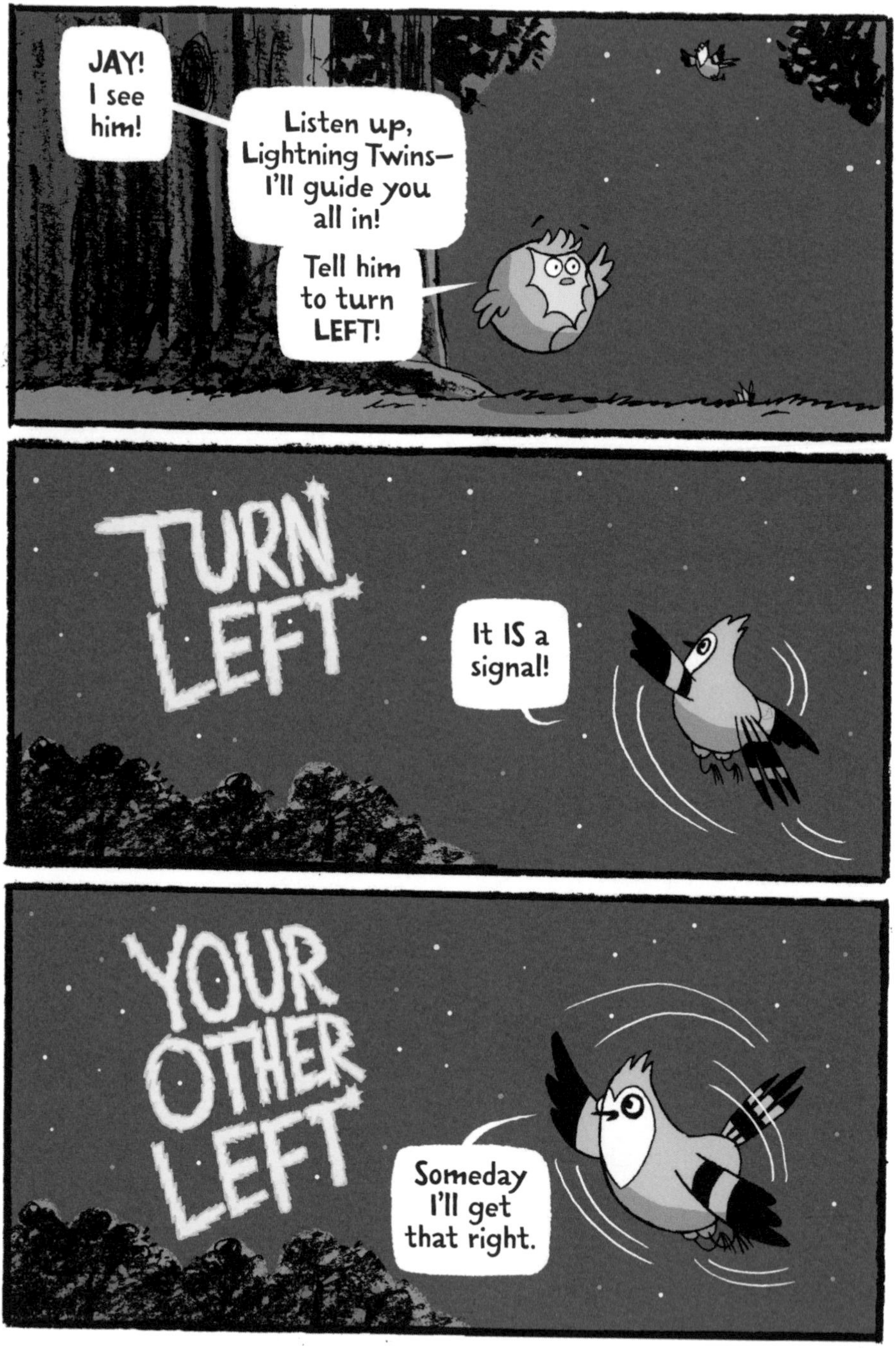
JAY! I see him!
Listen up, Lightning Twins— I'll guide you all in!
Tell him to turn LEFT!
TURN LEFT
It IS a signal!
YOUR OTHER LEFT
Someday I'll get that right.

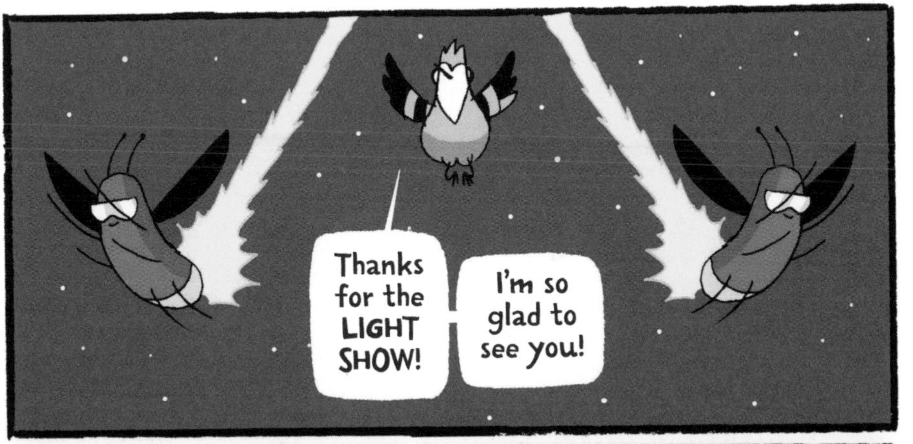
Thanks for the LIGHT SHOW!
I'm so glad to see you!

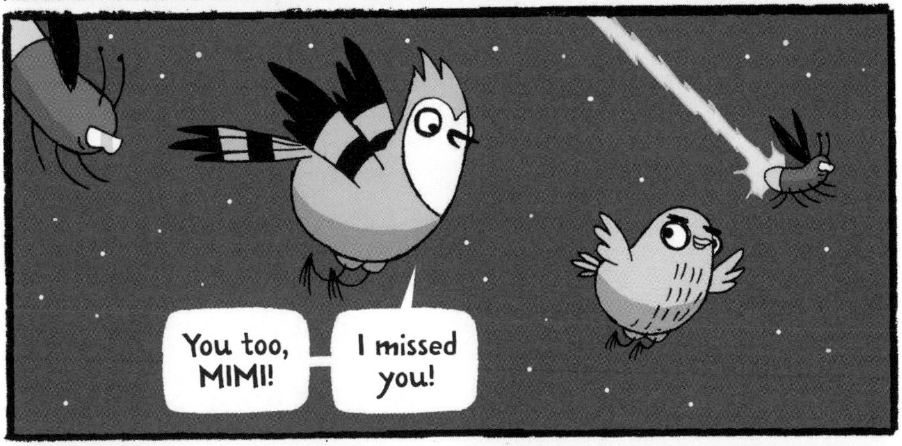
You too, MIMI!
I missed you!

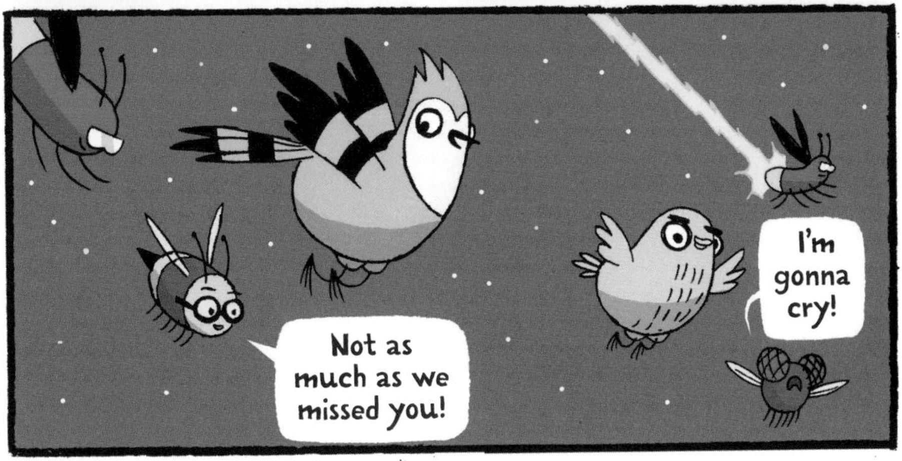
Not as much as we missed you!
I'm gonna cry!

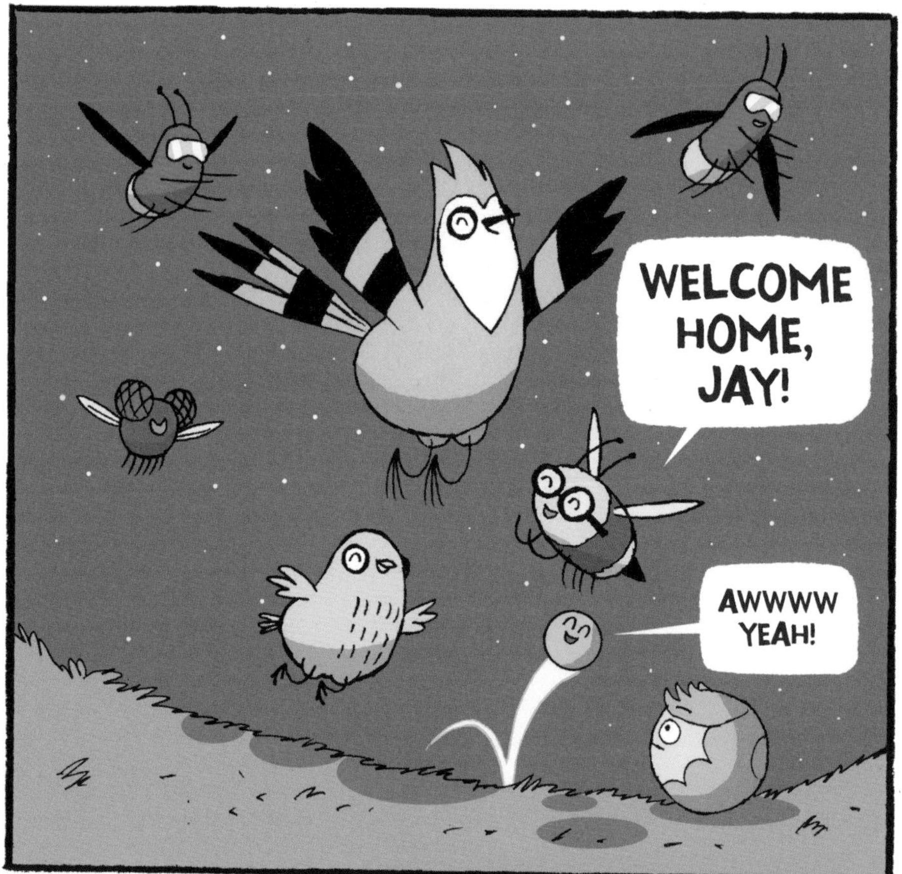
WELCOME HOME, JAY!
AWWWW YEAH!

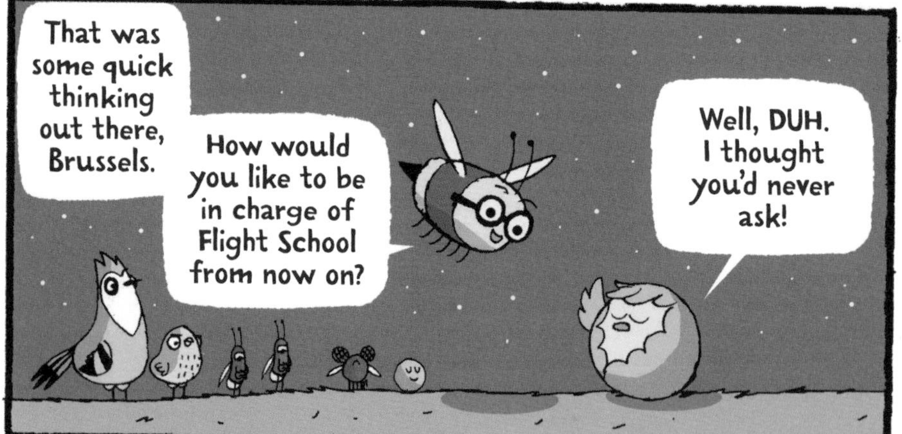
That was some quick thinking out there, Brussels.
How would you like to be in charge of Flight School from now on?
Well, DUH. I thought you'd never ask!

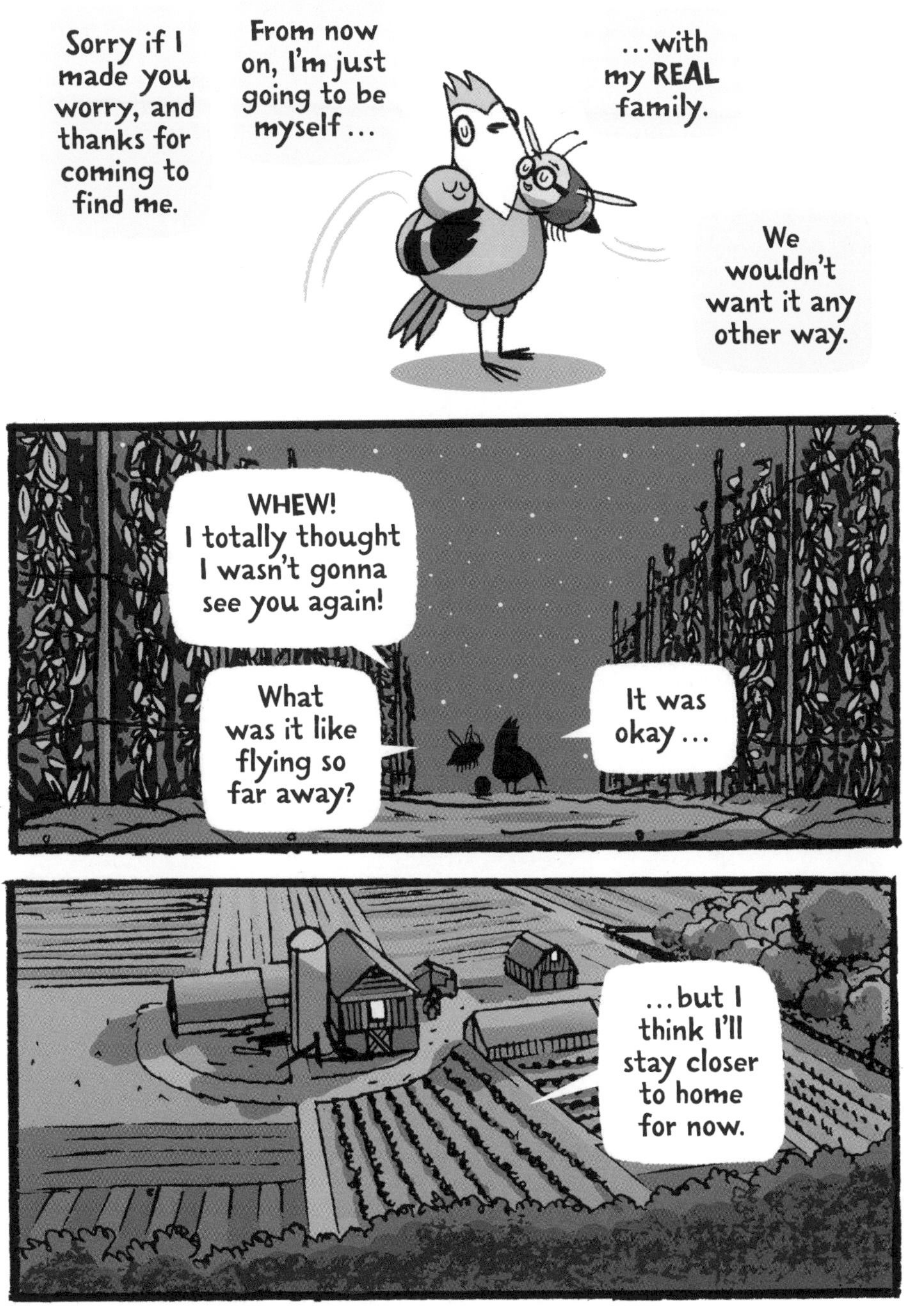

Sorry if I made you worry, and thanks for coming to find me.
From now on, I'm just going to be myself . . .
. . . with my **REAL** family.
We wouldn't want it any other way.
**WHEW!** I totally thought I wasn't gonna see you again!
What was it like flying so far away?
It was okay . . .
. . . but I think I'll stay closer to home for now.

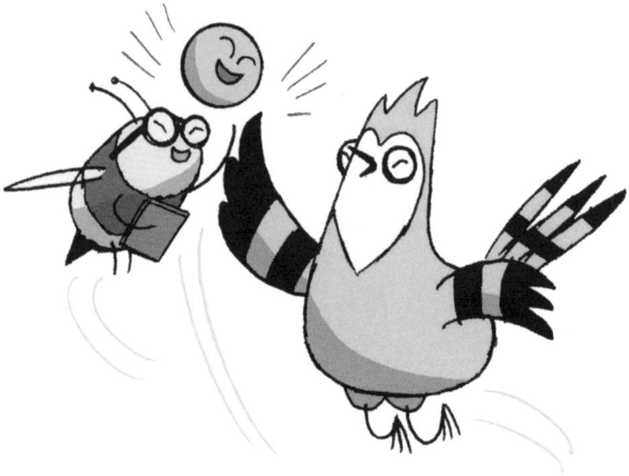

Thank you to Bret Parks, Juliet Parks, Elise Parks, Robin Parks, and Ssalefish Comics, without whom this book would not have been possible.

HarperAlley is an imprint of HarperCollins Publishers.

Pea, Bee, & Jay #3: Lift Off


Library of Congress Control Number: 2020949437
ISBN 978-0-06-298123-3 – ISBN 978-0-06-298122-6 (pbk.)

The artist used pencils, paper, a computer, and bee poop (lots and lots of bee poop) to create the digital illustrations for this book.
Typography by Erica De Chavez
21 22 23 24 25 GPS 10 9 8 7 6 5 4 3 2 1
❖
First Edition